# "Try your smooth lines somewhere else, Bo. I'm not buying any of it!"

"Lani, you're being childish. Wait a minute," Bo called after her, but she kept walking toward the hall. "Let's stop this playacting, shall we? I don't want anyone else. I want you."

"I want to believe you," Lani heard herself say.

"You can. I've never been more sure of anything in my whole life." His stare softened and Lani murmured a soft sigh of pleasure as she threw her arms around his neck, responding to her rising heartbeat and the ache she felt for him. She met his soft full lips with her own and was caught up in the bliss, recalling their passionate moments the night before.

Dear Reader:

June 1983 marks SECOND CHANCE AT LOVE's second birthday—and we have good reason to celebrate! While romantic fiction has continued to grow, SECOND CHANCE AT LOVE has remained in the forefront as an innovative, top-selling romance series. In ever-increasing numbers you, the readers, continue to buy SECOND CHANCE AT LOVE, which you've come to know as the "butterfly books."

During the past two years we've received thousands of letters expressing your enthusiasm for SECOND CHANCE AT LOVE. In particular, many of you have asked: "What happens to the hero and heroine after they get married?"

As we attempted to answer that question, our thoughts led naturally to an exciting new concept—a line of romances based on married love. We're now proud to announce the creation of this new line, coming to you this fall, called TO HAVE AND TO HOLD.

There has never been a series of romances about marriage. As we did with SECOND CHANCE AT LOVE, we're breaking new ground, setting a new precedent. TO HAVE AND TO HOLD romances will be heartwarming, compelling love stories of marriages that remain exciting, adventurous, enriching and, above all, romantic. Each TO HAVE AND TO HOLD romance will bring you two people who love each other deeply. You'll see them struggle with challenges many married couples face. But no matter what happens, their love and commitment will see them through to a brighter future.

We're very enthusiastic about TO HAVE AND TO HOLD, and we hope you will be too. Watch for its arrival this fall. We will, of course, continue to publish six SECOND CHANCE AT LOVE romances every month in addition to our new series. We hope you'll read and enjoy them all!

Warm wishes,

*Ellen Edwards*

Ellen Edwards
SECOND CHANCE AT LOVE
The Berkley Publishing Group
200 Madison Avenue
New York, N.Y. 10016

# Second Chance at Love

# CONQUERING EMBRACE
# ARIEL TIERNEY

### A SECOND CHANCE AT LOVE BOOK

CONQUERING EMBRACE

Copyright © 1983 by Ariel Tierney

Distributed by The Berkley Publishing Group

All rights reserved. No part of this publication may be reproduced or transmitted in any form or by any means, electronic or mechanical, including photocopy, recording, or any information storage and retrieval system, without permission in writing from the publisher.

Requests for permission to make copies of any part of the work should be mailed to: Permissions, Second Chance at Love, The Berkley Publishing Group, 200 Madison Avenue, New York, NY 10016.

First edition published June 1983

First printing

"Second Chance at Love" and the butterfly emblem are trademarks belonging to Jove Publications, Inc.

Printed in the United States of America

Second Chance at Love books are published by
The Berkley Publishing Group
200 Madison Avenue, New York, NY 10016

# 1

LEILANI NODDED TO the smiling security guard and, following the direction of his outstretched arm, swung her classic Mustang convertible past the studio entrance and found a parking spot next to the barnlike sound stage.

A quick glance into her rearview mirror assured her that, despite the hectic drive through San Diego's heavy weekend beach traffic, the liner around her blue eyes hadn't smudged and the light trace of pale pink lipstick on her full, curving lips still remained. Checking her watch, noting she was barely five minutes late, Lani grabbed her production notes, script, and a scratch pad and stretched her five-foot seven-inch frame out of the car.

Shaking out the wrinkles from her lightweight, lavender cotton dress, the lithe, deeply tanned twenty-nine year old hurried toward the sound stage entrance, her long chestnut locks fluttering in the warm, dry Santa Ana breeze.

Lani didn't particularly enjoy working Saturdays, but since her promotion to executive in charge of production for a prominent ad agency, it seemed to be the rule rather than the exception. Stepping through the large double doors, Lani hoped to get today's shoot over with as easily as possible. Maybe she'd still have time for an evening swim if they could wrap up before it got too late.

Inside, the cavernous stage was alive with bustling lighting, camera, and sound technicians. Lani was glad she'd chosen to wear sensible, slip-on flats as she gingerly stepped over a rats' nest of outstretched electrical cables and headed for the elegant living room "set," constructed ahead of her.

"Lani, thank goodness you're here. Where's Cornell?" She turned to see George Perry, director for today's filming, hurrying toward her, looking quite frazzled as he bit nervously on the end of his unlit cigar.

"You mean he's not here yet?" Lani answered as she took George's outstretched hand, shook it, and then watched bemusedly as the director raked a hand through his thoroughly mussed hair.

"That's right. I kinda hoped he was with you. If he doesn't show up soon, we'll run over our budget and you know what that'll cost."

Casting a quick glance around her, Lani could tell that everything was set and the crew was ready to begin, if their feature attraction ever showed up.

Problems, problems. Since she began overseeing the shooting of her clients' commercials it seemed like Lani had been plagued with setback after setback. Now she had a new one to deal with. She'd heard their "star" for today's commercial shoot, controversial San Diego pro-quarterback, Robert Cornell, was a character. His recent commercial for a leading brand of men's underwear had certainly generated a lot of amusing articles in the local gossip columns. Now she was beginning to understand why her fellow advertising execs at the agency had smirked when they learned of her assignment.

Slapping her things down on a nearby table, Lani once again checked her watch. "It's only been ten minutes, George, give it a little more time," she offered. Slumping into an empty director's chair, Lani picked up her production notes and, seeing George still hovering over her expectantly, she continued, "C'mon, George, I don't like it any more than you do, but you're making me nervous standing there like that..."

Loud barking suddenly punctuated the air and Lani and George both looked up to see a frazzled young female production assistant stumble into the stage, followed by a large, frisky golden retriever. "I think Mr. Cornell has arrived... ouch! Down!" the poor young woman blurted as the playful dog nipped at her heels, barking happily, having a great time.

Lani stood up and reached for the dog's trailing leash just as a well-formed, masculine hand suddenly appeared and grabbed it away from her. "Hold it, King. Fun's over boy," the accompanying voice called in amusement. Lani looked up to see an unkempt figure in rumpled clothing bending over, hugging the overgrown pup, laughing as if the commotion were a big joke.

"Bo Cornell?" George asked. The man stood up, eyed the director, and then offered a hand.

"You got it," he bellowed, while giving George's hand a hard, vigorous shake.

Lani couldn't believe her eyes. Here was the supposed heartthrob of pro football, standing before her wearing a filthy flannel shirt, muddy sneakers, and at least a couple of weeks of bushy, dark-brown beard. At just over six feet tall, he loomed like some kind of mountain man.

"Um, sorry I'm late. The coach gave the team an unexpected forty-eight hours of freedom. So I've been out fishing off of Mexico the last few days. I'd have been here on time except I hooked into a big one just before we got back in port. He must've fought me for forty-five minutes before he got away. But you know how it is." He laughed as if this fisherman's joke was perfectly acceptable.

Unable to contain her vexation any longer, Lani stepped in front of the man. "No, I don't know how it is, *Mr*. Cornell. Do you have any idea what it costs to keep a production crew waiting an extra fifteen minutes, on a weekend?"

For the first time Cornell turned directly to Lani, fixing piercing, deep hazel eyes on her. He stared intently into her own flashing blue ones, then raked his glance up and down her length in a quick, fluid appraisal. Finally, he broke into a broad grin. Lani felt as if he had quickly undressed her. Her initial indignation was replaced by a quickened pulse and a nervous tingling at the base of her spine. Despite his smile, his unrelenting stare seemed to burn into her.

"I guess I'm ignorant on that score, m'am. But, if I'd known I'd be keeping such a lovely creature as yourself waiting, I sure would've told the skipper to step on it." His backhanded apology was accompanied by a mischievous chuckle and Lani knit her brow in anger at his flippant attitude.

"Shall we skip the friendly chatter and get down to business?" She tried to sound firm, despite the nervous edge that suddenly seemed to grow at the back of her throat.

Cornell stared down at her, the corners of his teasing hazel eyes crinkling as he broadened his grin, showing perfect white teeth. "Well, that's what I'm here for. Who, by the way, do I have the pleasure of addressing?"

"Leilani Richards, and I happen to be in charge of this production." Lani tried to sound matter of fact, but her reply still came out rather officiously.

But, if Cornell noted her rising impatience, he evidently ignored it as he extended his hand toward her. "Then it is indeed a pleasure, ma'am."

# Conquering Embrace 5

Before she realized it, Cornell had taken her right hand in his, in a firm, yet somehow intimate grip. The warmth from his smooth palm seemed to radiate upward, through her arm, stirring Lani's pulse further as her heart beat faster and the downy hairs at the back of her slender neck prickled in sensual arousal.

Lani slowly withdrew her hand, suddenly aware of droplets of perspiration forming on her brow. Perhaps it was the hot stage lamps that made her notice the rising temperature. At least that's what she wanted to believe as Cornell continued to stare into her eyes. "Have you looked at the script?" she finally managed, breaking the momentary tension.

"Script... You mean for this little one-minute TV spot?" Cornell's response had a tinge of impatience, as if this whole affair were an annoying interruption to his vacation.

"It may not seem like such a big deal, Mr. Cornell, but scripts are essential even to a one-minute commercial. I can't expect you to fully understand that, but I suggest you study it while you get changed."

The gleam remained in his eyes as he continued to scrutinize Lani's growing anxiety. "I'm not a complete novice to these things. It's just that the last job I worked on didn't have any script, but then I doubt the producers were concerned with what I had to say." He laughed boisterously at this obvious reference to his underwear commercial.

Lani felt a crimson flush spread across her cheeks, not because of any embarrassment over Cornell's reference to his physical attributes, but because this mocking, jocular lout was having some fun at her expense. "Bobby, take our star's canine friend, will you," Lani called out to a nearby production assistant.

"Here you go, Bobby. King shouldn't cause you any trouble, he just likes to play a bit," Cornell said as he handed over the leash to the obliging young man. "If he gets bored waiting around, there's a soup bone out in my truck that should take care of him."

"Mary, Evan, will you show Mr. Cornell to his dressing room, and see if you can get him ready within the next half hour?" The hairdresser and wardrobe man responded to Lani's orders and were quickly at Cornell's side. Then, turning to the featured attraction, Lani tried to sound firm and businesslike. "We'll be here whenever you're ready, Mr. Cornell." She indicated the open door of the nearby dressing room with a sweep of her arm and sat down once again in the director's chair, snatching up her note pad and forcing herself to look away from Cornell's amused face.

"Whatever you say, m'am," he called out over his shoulder as Mary and Evan led him away. "Be back in a flash."

"Read the script," she yelled back at him, while beginning to pour over her production notes.

"Coffee, Lani?" Bobby asked before he stumbled and took a firmer hold on the leash as the golden retriever strained to follow his master.

"Sure, Bobby, thanks," Lani answered with a smile. She sank deeper into the chair, rubbing her slender fingers across her temples, hoping to stave off what seemed like an upcoming headache.

Lani took a sip of the steaming liquid before her, and tried to concentrate on her notes and the script. Her company's client for this commercial, a leading sherry producer, had stipulated that a name entity should be used to plug their product, hence Lani's firm's suggestion they use the well-known, San Diego football star, Cornell. She could see from the script that the commercial would be a mundane affair. It certainly wouldn't be one of her more challenging assignments, Lani thought, but it was for an important client. It was up to her to ensure the client's money was well spent and they'd be satisfied with her company's work. Hopefully, the part would be simple enough for the quarterback to handle. She only hoped he'd be serious and not ruin the whole thing. How typical of an athlete, she thought, as the sight of that loud, grizzled character still burned fresh in her memory. Like a puckish adolescent, he seemed to think the whole affair was a joke. Of course, what more could she expect from someone whose biggest care in the world was making sure an oval-shaped bladder was accurately thrown to any of a score of overpaid, thoroughbred receivers.

But as Lani's mind continued to dwell on him, her eyes blurred out the script in front of her and the image of his piercing hazel stare continued to appear. His eyes seemed to possess an intelligence all their own, apart from his slovenly exterior.

She closed the script and took another sip of the now tepid coffee, trying to turn her mind away from the mesmerizing image. But Lani's thoughts continued to center on him, tugging her emotions in a direction she'd hoped to avoid. A pang of nostalgia poked at her insides as the memory of another athlete from another time suddenly invaded her consciousness. Ken had exhibited the same carefree, flippant attitude toward responsibility that Cornell seemed to possess. Although it had been ten years since the star college hurdler had told Lani he had changed his mind about marrying her and wanted to pursue his hopes of making the Olympic team unhindered, the memory's bitter taste still lingered. Lani drained the styrofoam coffee cup and crushed it in her fingers.

She had just tossed the crumpled remains in a nearby waste can when the golden retriever perked up and yelped to announce the reappearance of his master.

Lani looked up to see Mary and Evan leave the dressing room followed by the gracefully striding Cornell. But instead of the bearded, slovenly mountain man, Lani stared wide-eyed at the freshly shaved, rugged features of an entirely different person. Wearing a black tuxedo and holding a folded script in one hand, Cornell walked right up to her, looking every bit like an elegant fashion plate.

"I hope you approve," he teased with a lazy grin.

Lani's nostrils caught the faint traces of an aromatic, masculine after-shave lotion. As Cornell spread his arms and turned nimbly for her perusal, Lani became aware once again of the rising warmth in the sound stage. He continued his mischievous smile until it became infectious and broke the momentary tension. As Lani's eyes traced the flairing lines of his grinning lips, she couldn't help but break into a smile of her own. Now it was her turn to scrutinize the preening figure before her with her own azure gaze.

His muscular yet trim upper body funneled down into a slim waist; his thighs tapered down, hard and smooth. Lani was surprised by his graceful physique, finding it nothing at all like the hulking monsters she'd thought were the rule in pro football.

Hoping not to betray her fascination, Lani winked back at him. "Oh, I suppose you'll do." Then, calling out to the huddled group of chatting technicians, "Okay, people, looks like we're ready to begin. George, our *star* has arrived." She delivered this last jibe with a little laugh, for Cornell's benefit, hoping he'd realize she wasn't the uncompromising taskmaster she'd first seemed. There was no sense in having him resent her for merely doing her job. She still didn't know if Cornell would be the typical on-camera prima donna. After having worked with her fair share, Lani knew the best way to get the job done was to make everyone as comfortable as possible.

It didn't take long, however, before Lani realized that Cornell was anything but a prima donna. As he rehearsed his lines and walked through the scene, following George's instructions, it became apparent that he was very professional. What's more, in the few minutes he'd taken to read the script in the dressing room, he'd thoroughly memorized his lines.

When they finally began shooting, Cornell was ready. However, it soon became obvious that the script was subpar, doing little to enhance the image of the client's product.

George, frantic as ever, was beside himself and when Lani finally decided they'd have to make some immediate changes, or call the whole afternoon a bust, she was surprised to find Cornell on her side. And what's more, he offered a few suggestions on dialogue changes, walking through the scene in demonstration, and markedly improved an otherwise bland commercial.

In between takes, Cornell was pleasant and lighthearted, joking with the technicians, playing with his dog, generally trying to ease everyone's frustration for having to work on a Saturday afternoon.

Maybe she was wrong about him, Lani mused as Cornell obviously had things under control. About halfway through the shooting, Bobby, the relatively new production assistant, knocked over a high-intensity light standard, ruining the shot as a resounding *crack* was accompanied by a shower of glass. George bit his cigar clean through. Bobby was obviously distraught and, even though it was a fairly common mistake, Lani could tell the young man was upset. Cornell had also noticed this and, shaking the bits of broken glass from his tuxedo, he consoled the young production assistant. Lani couldn't help being impressed with the sight of Cornell, coaxing George to settle down, then putting an arm about Bobby's shoulders and offering an account of when he was an eager college freshman, trying out for the team, only to make an embarrassing, boneheaded play. In contrast to her earlier judgment, Lani was impressed with Cornell's polished maturity.

Something else came across during the shooting that impressed Lani even more. As written, the script gave, at best, a perfunctory promotion for the rich, expensive wine. But when Cornell read it, going through the motions on the set, he added a touch of natural charm. He managed to convince her that he enjoyed the client's product. There was no doubt Cornell's grace projected throughout the stage and Lani hoped it would also come across on film. Could this be the same man who got such a wild reputation while filming an underwear commercial?

"Finally—all right folks, it's a wrap," George yelled, and a chorus of sighs went up throughout the stage. The technicians began striking the set and packing up their gear.

Cornell, brandishing a freshly opened bottle of the featured product, interrupted. "Friends, I've determined that the stuff I've just promoted so highly, is the real thing. How about a toast for a good day's work?" Several people voiced agreement to the proclamation and Cornell passed out styrofoam cups and poured a round for everyone.

With the toast concluded and Cornell back in the dressing room, Lani started to gather her things when George sauntered over to her, unwrapping a fresh cigar and striking a wooden match. "What do you think, Lani? Will the boss be satisfied?" George mumbled as he rolled the end of the cigar over the flaming match.

"You're the expert, George, but if it comes across on film anywhere near like it did live, I'd say you've got nothing to worry about."

Looking at his watch, George continued. "We even got the thing over with on time. I can't believe it. Say, the next time you've got a job with Cornell doing the promo, let me know, okay?"

"You'll be the first, George," Lani responded while jotting down a few quick notes on her pad. A cool, wet sensation suddenly grazed Lani's ankle and, after jumping back with a start, she looked down to see King, Cornell's overgrown pup, innocently panting up at her, having bussed her leg with his wet nose.

"You do that to all the girls you meet?" she teased as she bent down and scratched the affectionate animal behind the ears. Then, noting it had been a good six hours since they started this afternoon, Lani looked into the dog's friendly face. "I bet you're dying for a drink, huh, fella?" She found a discarded cup, went to the nearby water cooler, and filled it before kneeling down and offering the dog a drink. He responded instantly, sticking his nose deep into the cup, lapping thirstily, quickly draining the water.

"Well, King, looks like you found a new friend." Cornell was suddenly kneeling down beside Lani, giving the dog an affectionate pat on the head. Startled by his unexpected nearness, Lani looked up to see Cornell's rugged, tanned features a scant few inches from her face. His glinting hazel eyes stared intently at her and, feeling his breath warmly caress her cheeks, Lani was unable to tear her eyes from his mesmerizing gaze.

Meanwhile, King had grown impatient with licking the now-empty cup and, with a quick little bark, he moved toward Lani and began licking her face with his gentle but thoroughly wet tongue.

"My sentiments exactly." Cornell laughed as the playful beast continued his wet assault on Lani's cheeks.

Caught off guard by the dog's sudden movement, Lani found herself unable to keep her balance and was soon sprawled on her backside.

Cornell grabbed King by the collar. "Down, boy, c'mon..." and he pulled the dog away. Reaching down, Cornell placed a gentle, yet firm hand under Lani's arm and smoothly helped her to her feet. "Sorry about that. I guess he's still a bit of a pup," he offered while attempting to brush the dust off the back of Lani's dress.

Lani quickly stepped back, slightly flushed, embarrassed from her awkward fall. "It's all right, no harm done," she managed, shaking out the wrinkles in her dress and running a hand lightly through her dark, chestnut locks.

None of her movements were lost on Cornell as he lingered close to her, focusing all his attention on Lani's slender, well-proportioned body. "I can't say much for my dog's manners, Miss Richards, but there's nothing wrong with his taste in women." His remark was accompanied by a silly grin as he lazily folded his arms across his chest. Having shed the tuxedo, Cornell stood before her in faded jeans and a worn but clean V-necked T-shirt. Only the filthy sneakers remained of the grizzled mountain man she'd encountered earlier.

"I take it that's a compliment?"

"Of course," he replied. "But I would have thought someone like you would get enough of them to be able to tell the difference," Cornell continued with a note of challenge in his voice.

"That sounds like a practiced line if I ever heard one. Surely you can be more original than that, Mr. Cornell."

"Bo."

"What?"

"Bo. It's my nickname. You know Robert...Bo? Somewhere along the line a friend got the idea that Bo Cornell had a ring to it. I didn't much care at the time, but my friend, who is a sports reporter, began using it in his articles and it just stuck...Well?"

"Well, what?" Lani countered.

"You're supposed to offer in return that it's all right for me to address you by your first name."

"I'm not so sure it's wise to get too familiar, after all. Technically, I'm your boss. This kind of thing might make your motives seem suspect, don't you think." Now it was Lani's turn to challenge the grinning quarterback.

But, instead of responding to her question directly, Cornell simply threw back his head and laughed, as if he were mocking her. He finally continued, "I should have thought my motives, as you put it, were perfectly clear."

What kind of off-the-wall remark was that, Lani wondered, knitting her brow, reminded once again of the tremendous egos that Cornell, and most athletes, possess.

Before their "discussion" could continue, two female production secretaries and the camera operator appeared

# Conquering Embrace

and corralled Cornell. As the girls gushed over him, asking for autographs, and the cameraman asked about tickets to an upcoming game, Lani decided she'd had enough chitchat and walked away.

Lani quickly conferred with George, making arrangements to get the film back from the lab, edited, and sent to the agency according to their predetermined schedule.

Outside the sound stage, walking toward her car, Lani noted the intense, orange, red, and blue sunset. She guessed she'd skip her usual ocean swim. Somehow she just didn't have the energy. Reaching her car, Lani tossed her things into the back seat and decided to leave the top down. It was a beautiful evening and she hadn't realized until now how stifling it could be inside a locked sound stage, working with intense lamps blazing away.

The warm Santa Ana breeze continued to blow its desert air out to sea and, for a moment, Lani stood by her car, letting the wind whip through her hair, thoroughly enjoying the sensation. Even though the seasonal wind kept the temperature near ninety degrees, it was dry and clean, giving this autumn evening an almost surreal quality.

Lani had opened the door to the Mustang and started to get in when she felt a presence behind her. She turned quickly and her heart nearly skipped a beat when she saw Cornell standing there. Lani sucked in a deep breath, almost a gasp, in reaction to his sudden appearance.

Managing to compose herself, Lani narrowed her eyes in anger at this intrusion. "You enjoy sneaking up on women in the dark?" she demanded.

"I didn't mean to scare you," he offered apologetically, "although I wouldn't consider it dark just yet."

"I don't care to play word games and, as you can see, I'm on my way out, so, if you'll excuse me..."

"Wait, I just wanted to ask if you'd like to join me for dinner."

Having started to get in the car, Lani stopped and turned toward Cornell, surprised by his directness. After a moment of scrutiny, deciding his nonchalant grin indicated he thought she was a pushover, she grinned back at him. "No, thanks, but I suspect you'll have better luck with one of your fans," she offered, nodding her head in the direction of the two production secretaries, waving to Cornell as they walked across the parking lot toward their cars.

Once again Lani reached for the car door handle but Cornell pushed it away from her, slamming the door shut. As she turned back to him, ready to spit out her anger, Cornell stepped closer and his smoldering hazel eyes flashed his intensity.

"I think you've got me all wrong, Miss Richards." His tone was measured, controlled. "I can't deny I'm physically attracted to you, but there's more to me than that."

Lani was surprised by his sudden forcefulness and was at a loss for words as her eyes focused on his flaring lips. Finally dropping her gaze from his face, she found herself tracing the line of his jaw, down his smooth throat, settling her eyes on the wisp of thick, dark hair that protruded from the collar of his shirt. Despite the tense confrontation, Lani realized a warmth was building in the pit of her stomach, spreading across her slender thighs. She quickly put a hand behind her and tried to steady herself against the car.

As if he sensed her growing nervousness, Cornell softened his tone. Then placing his finger beneath her downturned chin, he gently lifted her gaze to meet his.

"I only wanted to say that I appreciate a well-run production. I got the idea that I could benefit from your expertise in the advertising field and maybe we could discuss it over dinner. Believe me, I wasn't looking for just another conquest."

Lani noted the sincerity in his voice and, her curiosity piqued, she leaned back against the car and folded her arms. "Go on, Bo, how might you benefit from my expertise?"

## Conquering Embrace 15

"I've been playing an awful long time now and I know I'll have to retire pretty soon. I'm only thirty-eight. Pretty young actually in the business world, but as far as football goes, I'm past being a veteran; I'm an old man. I've managed to spread my name around and it's safe to say that most sports fans have heard of Bo Cornell."

It wasn't often that a celebrity, let alone an athlete, could be so honest about passing his prime, Lani reflected. It certainly hadn't been her experience to hear them be so frank. Remembering the rumors about the underwear commercial, she teased, "Yes, even I've heard of your exploits, although the accounts weren't exactly about your achievements on the field."

"You must mean my debut in my skivvies. That's exactly what I'm talking about. Today was my second commercial and if everything works out, my name and only slightly battered face should be a marketable item."

"I think I see what you're getting at," Lani interjected. "You'd like me, or better yet, my firm, to help promote your reputation, is that it?"

"Sort of, although I generally consider ad agencies as trend stealers rather than trend setters. Most firms run around talking about finding new approaches to appeal to the public, but in reality they simply rehash the same old stuff time and again."

Lani couldn't help smiling at this quip. Cornell certainly had most of her associates well pegged. "What makes you think I'm any different?" she challenged.

His green-brown eyes took on a liquid hue and his voice grew husky. "Maybe you're not, but I liked the way you handled yourself and your production. Besides, I doubt the typical ad exec has such lovely deep blue eyes."

Again, Lani said nothing, turning her gaze away.

"What do you say, is it worth a quiet, guaranteed delicious meal for your thoughts on the matter?"

Lani couldn't deny this man had charm. In fact, he exuded the type of controlled confidence that her boss had always stressed during their casting sessions. Perhaps Cornell was a diamond in the rough, Lani considered, and, with just the right amount of polish perhaps she could turn him into a real commercial draw. She knew her boss wouldn't be adverse to her signing a celebrity such as this dashing quarterback for their firm, especially if she could convince him that this rugged, personable "hunk" could, with a thorough cleaning up of his act, become a marketable personality. Bo could generate a bit of money, both for the agency and for herself.

The thought of playing a Professor Higgins to Bo's Eliza Doolittle intrigued Lani and with a sly little smile, she finally replied, "Why not, besides, I'm starved."

Cornell's mouth broadened into a wide grin. "Wonderful. I'll need about an hour to drop off King and change. I'll pick you up then, okay?"

"Sounds good," she replied as Cornell started to lean toward her. Lani's heart began to beat faster as she focused on his lips moving closer. But, at the last second, Cornell bent from the waist, in mock chivalry, and lightly grazed her hand with a kiss. It was a corny move but a wave of pulsing, tingling electricity seemed to shoot up her arm. She quickly grabbed a pencil from her purse and jotted down her address for him.

"Au revoir," he said, straightening up and striding across the parking lot toward a battered, muddied pickup truck.

Lani stepped into her own car and, after starting it with a brief roar from the quiet, powerful engine, she turned her head and called out to him. "Lani!"

"What?" he yelled back.

"My first name . . . in its familiar form," she answered as she pulled the Mustang past his truck and headed out of the parking lot. In her rearview mirror she could see Bo smiling in response before joining King in the cab.

As she drove toward home, the breeze sent her hair flying behind her and Lani was filled with heady excitement. Although she wasn't quite sure what she'd agreed to in accepting Bo's invitation, her heart beat fast and strong and the back of her hand still tingled from his kiss.

# 2

THE ELEVATOR ROSE with a smooth, quiet efficiency and Lani and Bo both shifted their feet uneasily as they rode toward the restaurant at the top of the tall office building. Lani couldn't help smiling as she noted that both of them were caught offguard by the car's sudden lurch upward. Bo's eyes crinkled in response to Lani's smile.

"I'll never get used to these things," he commented. "Can you imagine getting stuck in one of these sardine cans?"

"Please, don't even *think* it," Lani replied. "It happened to me once. The power went out and I was stuck, alone in the dark, for nearly two hours."

A wicked smile played across Bo's lips. "Of course, you wouldn't be alone now...I'm sure we could find some way to pass the time."

Lani looked up with a start but when she saw Bo having a difficult time keeping a straight face, she feigned annoyance. With a hand on her hip, she said, "Slow down, tiger, you don't want to get called for a penalty."

Bo threw back his head and laughed, but the smooth, sudden stop of the elevator stiffled his amusement. The doors opened, Bo took her arm, and they stepped into the lowlit elegance of Mr. A's restaurant.

This was a business meeting, she kept telling herself but, turning her head and gazing at Bo's rugged features, Lani felt a nervous tingling on the arm Bo gently held as they approached the waiting maître d'.

Lani quickly switched her attention to her dress, running a hand across the skirt of the knee-length, creamy white silk, making sure there were no wrinkles from the ride in the cab of Bo's pickup. Then she gently patted her hand across her dark hair, making sure no tendrils had escaped from the back of her head, where it was pinned up, accentuating her curving, slender neck. With her slim, matching high-heeled sandals enhancing her lean but well-shaped legs, Lani realized she wasn't exactly dressed for business. Nevertheless, she liked the way the creamy silk contrasted with her deep tan. Even in business, Lani reminded herself, one does best when feeling and looking their best. She unconsciously fingered one of the pink, angel-skin coral earrings that dangled from the gold fitting at her earlobe.

"Hello, Bo, how ya doing?" The maître d' greeted them with a smile as he recognized the quarterback.

"Just fine, Johnny," Bo answered, clapping a hand on the young man's shoulder. "John, I'd like you to meet Leilani Richards," Bo offered, moving Lani forward for the man's perusal.

"A pleasure," Johnny replied with a slight nod of his head to Lani and a knowing wink to Bo, obviously acknowledging Lani's attractiveness. "Usual table, Bo?" he continued, grabbing a couple of menus.

"That'll be fine," Bo answered while reaching into the pocket of his camel hair sport coat and producing a couple of tickets which he pressed into Johnny's hand.

"San Diego versus Washington. Hey, thanks, Bo. I knew you'd come through," Johnny replied gratefully, while directing them toward a corner table, next to a large glass window overlooking downtown San Diego. As Johnny held the chair for her, Lani was aware that Bo seemed to get on with everyone. This easygoing, fluid charm, which she first noted during their commercial shoot, was something that came naturally to him and something that could certainly work in their favor in making him a marketable celebrity.

She gazed out the huge window and took in the magnificent view of San Diego's skyline spreading out around them. The city winked and glittered. Shifting her gaze off to the distance, she saw a tiny, bobbing light indicating a boat gliding through the harbor.

Turning back to Bo, Lani saw him staring at her, obviously enjoying himself.

"Not a bad view, don't you think?" he asked, reading her mind.

"You could say that," Lani agreed. "I take it you come here often?"

"Oh, every now and then. The scampi's particularly good and besides, I like the crowd they draw here. They get a fair share of football fans but not the crazy nuts who constantly bother you for an autograph or to get them tickets, you know what I mean."

"What about Johnny. You didn't seem to mind giving him tickets," Lani stated, wondering how serious Bo really was in wanting to escape the public's eye.

"Well, there's always an exception," Bo shrugged, "but Johnny's been a good friend for some time. It's hard to find a place where you can relax and not worry about being hassled by fans. Even though San Diego's a big town, it's not always easy to find some privacy when you need it," Bo lamented as he picked up the wine list and scanned what vintages the restaurant had to offer.

As the little glass-encased candle on the table flickered, Lani studied the glimmering reflections it cast across the sculpted contours of Bo's face. Did this mean he didn't crave the adoration of the screaming masses who usually flocked to America's favorite pastime? If so, this was certainly a new twist. It seemed that every athlete she'd ever met, including her former boyfriend, had needed the ego boost of the cheering mobs and the autograph hounds.

"You realize, Bo, that the public ultimately pays your salary and it's them you'll have to please if you hope to continue as a draw after your playing days are over," Lani suggested, gauging to see if he was aware of this very important fact.

He looked up from the wine list and Lani caught an emerald glint in his eyes as the candlelight continued its flickering.

"No, m'am, I guess I can't forget that. But don't get me wrong. I love the fans. In fact, I've found few things in life that can match the feeling I get when I connect on a long bomb and suddenly there's fifty thousand people screaming my name. It really sends the adrenaline pumping." Bo leaned close, placing his elbows on the table, and gazed intently into her eyes. "It's not just the screaming fans that get me off, though, Lani. There's something special about being an athlete." He took a moment to reflect on his words, composing his thoughts, continuing to stare intently at her.

Pulling her gaze away, Lani noticed his graceful, yet masculine hands turning a large diamond and gold ring around one finger.

"It's just a little token really," he began, following her look. "It's a prize from the Super Bowl win last year. I'm not really after rings or the other awards. It's nothing so concrete. Just getting out on the field, using my God-given skills, putting everything I have, everything I am, on the line and going all out is the real thrill. Even if a pass falls incomplete... or we fumble, it's not that big a deal. But when everything goes right, when every little nuance of a performance comes together and I see a man

# Conquering Embrace 23

sprint down the field and catch my best pass and score... the feeling is incredible. That's really the ultimate thrill. I'm not sure the fans can understand that, but it doesn't matter in the end. To have competed and done my best is where it's at for me, Lani, it's what I strive for." His eyes flashed intently with the proclamation before he eased back in his chair.

"I think I know what you mean, Bo," Lani offered, impressed with his sincerity. Seeing his eyes arch in surprise, she continued, "I was a bit of an athlete myself. I was one of the top twenty women collegiate tennis players. I'd flirted with the idea of turning pro, but I got turned off sports for a while and put all my energy into fashioning a business career." The memory of Ken's moody selfishness and his eventual betrayal washed over Lani, and she hesitated for a moment before continuing. "I know what it's like to put in the endless hours of work, going over the same strokes over and over again. Sometimes I thought my arm would fall off. I got so tired and frustrated, I even broke down and cried. But when the time came for a match, and I had to put all that preparation on the line... and then see it pay off with a clean winning shot at match point, it really is the ultimate feeling, the real payoff for all that hard work."

A smile tugged at the corners of Bo's mouth. "I thought you must be into something physical..."

"What do you mean?"

"Well, judging from those curvy legs, I figured you had to be into athletics of some sort or another... It's obvious all that hard work paid off, Lani." He punctuated the remark with a teasing wink.

Self-consciously, Lani gazed at her legs, seeing them stretched tanned, catlike from beneath the soft furls of her full skirt. Then, lifting her gaze, she saw Bo staring at them with the same silly grin and now it was her turn to try and keep a straight face. Without saying a word, she drew her legs primly together beneath the table.

Despite the overt nature of Bo's rather corny flirtations, the compliment made Lani's pulse race. Her legs did indeed look great and she'd known for some time that all the hours she put into her tennis game, to say nothing of the considerable time she spent swimming in the ocean, were well worth it when they paid such handsome benefits. Feeling a flush spread across her cheeks, she averted her gaze from his probing stare, determined that this dashing jock had better keep his mind on business.

"Here you go, Bo, Lani, compliments of the house."

Lani turned to see Johnny arrive at their table, holding forth a bottle of white wine and carrying two long-stemmed wineglasses in his other hand.

"I know you like Chardonnay, Bo, so I saved this one for you. It's still a bit young, but not a bad little wine at all." Johnny casually offered the assessment as he effortlessly drew out the cork and poured a sampling into Bo's glass. Bo sniffed, swirled the liquid around, and then took a small sip. Lani was grateful for the break in their conversation. It seemed the more Bo directed his attention to her the more she felt his magnetism. How could she possibly work with the man under these circumstances? And, was it work she was most interested in now?

For the next hour, the dinner meeting went pleasantly. As Bo had said, the scampi was excellent. With the food taking most of their attention, their conversation stayed on fairly safe ground. Lani went over a few basic rules she felt Bo should understand. They were simple things, such as never berating a sponsor's product, no matter how informal the situation. And he should keep his personal friendships beyond reproach, at least when reporters were around. Also, he should never sell the public short. Lani said she was sure Bo was aware of most of these, but she assured him it never hurt to be reminded.

When they had finished dinner, and sat back in their chairs with brandies in front of them, Bo and Lani forgot

## Conquering Embrace 25

about business for a while and Lani found herself at ease, speaking freely. She gazed at his finely structured hand wrapped around the brandy snifter as he took a sip of the aromatic liquor.

"So tell me, Lani," he began, taking the glass from his lips, "how does a tanned, tennis-playing ad exec wind up in San Diego, supervising commercials that feature dumb country boy quarterbacks?"

Lani gazed at her hand as she swirled the amber liquid around in the snifter. "I grew up in Hawaii, actually, and lived there until I started college. Sometimes I wish I were back, living the simple life, not worrying about the gripes of short-sighted sponsors, production deadlines, temperamental actors." She sipped the fiery liquid, tasting its smoky, deep flavor, feeling it slide down her throat to settle warmly in her stomach. She peered over the glass at Bo. He remained attentive, leaning his chin on his hands, his elbows on the table. "Don't get me wrong," she continued. "I like my job and I intend to go all the way with it. I like San Diego. It's a lot less crazy than L.A. and less congested than New York. I'm with a good company and I'd never be able to find the same opportunity in Hawaii, at least not in this field. It's just that when I was a little girl, I spent most of my time, the summers at least, swimming in the ocean, sailing, surfing, and just hanging out with my grandfather. It seemed so idyllic compared to the bustle of the city."

"I'm fond of the simple life myself, Lani," Bo offered. "I grew up on a farm in Kansas. Nothing so spectacular as Hawaii, I'm afraid, but I can still remember watching the sunrise sending the morning's first light across the waves and waves of wheat spread out across the flattest land you ever saw. Like waves of shimmering gold. It was pretty boring a lot of the time but every now and then, maybe when I was fishing with my dad or just running around with some of the other kids hunting frogs... things seemed so peaceful, so basic. It seemed like it was just me and the land, like we were friends almost. Sounds kind of silly, I guess." He smiled shaking his head and taking another sip.

"It doesn't sound silly at all," Lani countered. "My grandfather was a native Hawaiian, probably the wisest man I've ever known. He showed me things about nature that I'll never forget. He used to take me by the hand when I was only two years old, hold me up in the surf, and move my little arms and legs, showing me how to stroke. He taught me to swim while I could barely walk. I was scared, believe me. I must have been a couple of years older when he told me how the sea was the greatest thing in the world and of all the wonderful things there are, only the sea has remained uncontrolled by man. It has its own power, it's own integrity. But even though she gets a little crazy sometimes, if you respect her, the sea will let you enjoy her beauty, she'll talk to you, and she'll share all her treasures with you." Lani paused, fixing her gaze on her glass, smiling to herself. "My happiest memories are back on the islands, swimming, walking with granddad."

Bo studied her, as if he were tracing every feature. The warmth that flooded over Lani was not due only to the brandy. "And tell me, Miss Richards, where did you get such exotic blue eyes?"

"My grandmother was English," Lani replied, aware of the huskiness in Bo's voice. "... a strong woman who worked as a cook on a fishing trawler before she met my grandfather and decided to marry him. It really shocked her family, very improper you know." She giggled attempting to mimic a stuffy British accent. Lani could still picture the gray-haired, regal woman, accompanying Lani and granddad sometimes on their long walks through the lush rain forests of Hawaii.

"And what about you, Lani? Has Mr. Right come your way yet?" Bo queried, his eyes riveted on her.

Shaken by his directness, Lani stared down at the tablecloth, composing herself, wondering how far to let

## Conquering Embrace 27

Bo steer the conversation. "No, I guess not. I thought maybe he had once, but..." Her voice trailed off.

Across the table, Bo emptied his snifter and an attractive waitress was at his side almost as soon as the glass touched the table. Lani stared at the woman nonplussed. The waitress asked if Bo was ready for another and when he nodded, Lani caught a brief but obvious eye communication between them. From Bo's smiling reply it seemed he was aware of the waitress' flirtations.

Lani guessed this sort of thing happened often and Bo seemed to take it in stride. Lani had always heard that pro athletes had more than their share of female admirers, but she'd never been around jocks in their hunting grounds. She wondered if Bo considered this type of fan attention a drawback to his trade... or an added bonus.

"Well?" Bo asked, turning his attention back to Lani.

"There's not much to tell, really, Bo. I was engaged to a man when I was in college and it didn't work out, that's all." Lani tried to sound matter of fact but the memory of her affair with Ken still churned her up inside and she had to tear her face away from Bo's probing stare.

After a few moments, he settled back in his chair. "Well, I haven't met the right woman either, up until now, anyway." Bo's eyes took on that same teasing glint.

His charm was infectious and Lani couldn't help smiling at his reference to their date tonight.

"I'm not a prude or anything, don't get me wrong, I've had my share of affairs."

"And what constitutes your fair share? A couple, a dozen, an even gross?" Now it was Lani's turn to tease and she took full advantage of the opportunity.

Bo frowned, only mildly amused. "I never keep score, at least off the field. Beneath all this worldly exterior beats the heart of a simple country boy lucky enough to be able to throw a funny looking ball eighty yards on the fly."

"A talent we hope will make you a long-lasting household name," Lani added as the waitress sauntered over with Bo's brandy. To Lani's surprise, the woman lingered over the table, staring at Bo, and flashing a smile that was more than just friendly.

"Excuse me for staring, but you're Bo Cornell, aren't you? It's kinda neat to see you in the flesh." The waitress virtually gushed.

"Um, thanks, Miss..." Bo smiled pleasantly, unable to ignore her attention.

"My name's Carol, Bo. You suppose I could get your autograph? I collect them." Before he had a chance to answer, she tore a page from her order pad and placed it, with a pen, in front of Bo.

"Sure, anything you say, Carol," he replied obligingly. He finished and handed the paper back to the woman.

Lani could hardly believe her eyes as she saw the woman slyly slip a small card into Bo's breast pocket. They exchanged knowing smiles before she moved away from the table.

"Thank you so much, Bo. Maybe we'll run into each other again sometime," she hinted suggestively.

"Could be, Carol," he answered before turning his attention back to Lani. He waited until the woman flounced off. "Sorry about that, Lani. I guess these interruptions come with the territory, although I shouldn't complain. I should only be so lucky that people will still want my autograph *after* I retire."

Something in his cocky tone grated on Lani's nerves. That would-be groupie just slipped him her phone number and here he was, talking with another woman, like he was juggling them in the air. Lani's blood was beginning to boil.

"Lani... anything wrong?" Bo asked after a few moments of silence.

Twisting the napkin on her lap, Lani fought for control in her voice. "Nothing, Bo, nothing at all. What makes you ask?" Even though she tried to sound matter of fact,

## Conquering Embrace

Lani knew Bo could sense her sarcasm.

Rubbing his chin, Bo seemed to be doing a ham actor's job of pretending to be puzzled. "I hope you're not upset because of that girl, the waitress?"

Lani said nothing but Bo had to be aware of the darts she was sending from her flashing blue eyes.

When she didn't say anything, he continued in an even tone, "That sort of thing happens to me all the time, although it's the first time it's happened here. I get so used to people coming up and asking for autographs, I don't give it much thought really. They are the fans right, the ones who keep me in the meat and potatoes? Like you said, Lani, the public is ultimately who makes or breaks you in this business." He reached across the table, lightly grasping Lani's chin between his thumb and forefinger and tilting her eyes to meet his.

Lani tried to avoid looking at him, but the tenderness of his touch and his inquisitive stare drew her to him like a moth to a flame. Her eyes traced the strong line of his jaw, upward, across his tan, smooth cheeks. His slightly musky scent wafted past Lani's nose, sending a shiver through her whole body. For a moment, Lani was caught fast in her own swirling senses. She finally managed to lean away, out of Bo's grasp, unsure of her mixed feelings for this man. "I think it's time to bring this thing to a close. I'd really like to go home, if you don't mind, Bo." Without waiting for an answer, Lani finished her brandy and picked up her purse.

"Whatever you say," Bo conceded. He stood up and reached over to help her with her chair. "I hope you liked the scampi."

"It was great, just great," Lani said, trailing Bo in her wake as he hurriedly dug into his pockets for some bills to put on the table.

On the bouncy ride back in the cab of Bo's fourwheel drive pickup, Lani and the quarterback hardly exchanged a word. She rolled down the window and with the warm breeze blowing through the cab, she leaned back against the headrest, her eyes closed, trying to lose herself to the rhythmic bounce of the heavy vehicle on its stiff springs.

The truck drew to a stop and Bo turned off the engine. Lani opened her eyes to see the familiar white stucco and tile front of her Spanish courtyard condominium.

Lani put her hand on the door handle but hesitated for a second.

"Lani, will you have lunch with me tomorrow?" Bo asked, loping an arm across her seat, behind her shoulders.

"I'm busy tomorrow," Lani replied, relieved that she didn't have to make up a lie. "I'm entered in a tennis tournament at my club."

"Hmm, what about breakfast then?" Bo's suggestive tone was accompanied by a leer.

His arrogance stabbed at Lani like a hot needle and she could no longer contain her feelings. "What is it that makes you jocks think women are such pushovers? Where do you get off thinking I'd care to fall into your arms without a second thought, as if I should consider myself lucky to catch the gold-plated attention of a superstar?" She spat out the last word as if it were poison.

Bo's smile faded and he backed off slightly. "I don't understand, Lani. I thought we had a nice time tonight. I got the idea we got on well together."

"Is that why you let that groupie slip you her phone number?" Lani challenged, staring hard at him.

"Groupie? You mean the waitress? You mean this?" Bo asked as he reached into his coat pocket and retrieved the card.

"Of course that's what I mean," Lani fumed. "I can't believe you actually let her put that in your pocket, with me sitting across the table from you, and you acting as if there wasn't a thing wrong in the world." Lani shook her head still dumbfounded by his move. "Is that the way you deal with your women; letting them stand in line, giving them your witty lines just for a chance to have a fling with the great Bo Cornell?"

"But I get these things all the time," he replied, surprised by Lani's attitude. "It's bad enough when the team is in town, but on the road, the hotels are crawling with what you call groupies. It's more of a hassle to turn them down than it is to just accept their numbers and then toss them away later." He held the little card in front of her and tore it into pieces before tossing the remains out his window, where they fluttered away in the breeze.

His explanation sounded convincing, but Lani felt her heart beating hard in her chest. She needed to get away from him and sort out her feelings. Her hand moved to grab the door handle.

"Hold on a minute, Lani. I don't want you to run away with the wrong impression," he coaxed.

"Let's forget it, all right, Bo? We had a simple business dinner. We discussed business and now the meeting's over. If it's okay with you, I'm going to bed, to sleep, *alone*." She pulled on the door handle but the door wouldn't open. She yanked on it again, getting more and more anxious. "What's wrong with this darn door? Why won't it open?" she blurted, angry, frustrated.

"Wait a minute, Lani, I'll get it." Bo got out of the truck quickly and walked around to her door.

As he set himself and tugged with two hands, Lani exhaled and looked upward, musing on the irony of his stupid truck holding her prisoner.

His first effort proved useless and he set himself again. "This door's never been the same since I slid this side of the truck into a tree. Sometimes it takes just the right... little... tug... there, she's free."

Lani heard a distinct click and Bo swung the door open. She quickly stepped down and started to walk off.

"Lani?" Bo called out as she moved away at a brisk pace. Lani was determined not to answer him, having said all she intended to.

A strong hand grasped her wrist firmly as Bo stopped her in her tracks. He turned her around to face him.

"Lani, I don't want you to be angry with me," he said, pressing her against him, his face a scant few inches from hers, his eyes intently searching. The warmth of Bo's body sent Lani's senses reeling and she turned her face away.

With her pulse racing, Lani fought for control in her voice. "Let's call it an evening, all right. I'm tired and it's late."

But he grabbed her chin and turned her head, forcing her to look at him. "Lani, you can't deny there's something happening between us. Why fight it?"

Bo's breath felt hot against her cheeks and for a moment Lani felt helpless, staring at his sculpted, curving lips, so near to her own. He started to lean closer and Lani, feeling her knees weaken, fought against the sensual magnetism radiating from him, unwilling to give in to his powerful allure. She needed time to think, time to understand why this man made her heart beat at such a terrible pace. "We're a long way from a football field, Bo, and I don't feel like being tackled. Thanks for dinner," she said with finality, squirming from his grasp. He relaxed his grip and Lani felt relief as she started toward her condo.

"I'd like to keep in touch. I'll call you, Lani," Bo responded shrugging his straight, broad shoulders.

"Sure, but make it at the office, during business hours. My secretary will give me any messages," Lani replied coldly. Walking through the courtyard toward her apartment, Lani looked back over her shoulder and saw Bo looking after her, hands on hips, seeming bewildered. She felt the warm Santa Ana wind filtering through her silk dress, sending the fabric fluttering up and around her shapely legs. Even though she turned away from him, Lani knew Bo was still watching her, and she could literally feel his hazel eyes raking over her body.

# 3

LANI TUGGED AT the laces of her white tennis sneakers trying to concentrate on her upcoming match. Someone down the aisle from her slammed a locker's steel door and the clatter reverberated off the concrete floor, right through Lani's head. Determined to stay calm, she finished tying her second shoe with a sure, smart little bow, stood up, and walked to the mirror on a nearby wall. Tying her hair into a ponytail, she tried to sort out the events of the previous evening. It had been a long time since she had felt this way, a long time since she had been aroused by anyone. Slipping a white cotton sweatband over her forehead, Lani stood back from the mirror for a final look. Her short, one-piece, white tennis dress was functional, comfortable, and complimented her as an athlete, while in no way denying she was a lithe, attractive woman.

Even though she was prepared for the tournament and

looked self-assured, Lani felt butterflies fluttering in her stomach. Her thoughts continued to drift to Bo and his smouldering eyes, his full, curving lips, his well-formed, masculine hands holding her firmly against him.

A woman wrapped in a towel glided by still dripping water and trailing steam from the showers. Lani turned from the mirror, tossed two large-headed rackets into her gym bag, along with a towel and an extra sweatband. How ironic, she thought: After she had placed Ken and all he represented behind her, here she was again, in another locker room, caught up in her feelings for another jock. The familiar smells and sounds of the club's facility were the same as when she was in school, playing tennis, hanging around while Ken practiced.

Fishing in her bag for a Band-Aid, Lani wondered if somewhere in her experience with the star college hurdler there might be a hint of what lay in store for her with Bo. Images from the college yearbook came to mind. She'd worked on the publication and recalled pasting up photographs, including Ken's. One picture, a shot of him clearing the last hurdle in a conference championship meet, said it all. His sleek, sinewy body stretched in a fluid line, his face grim and determined. That was Ken.

How young she was, Lani mused, as she wrapped the Band-Aid around a tender spot on her ring finger. She thought he was so dashing and she loved it when he came to pick her up for a date. The other girls in the dorm used to get so excited when they saw him. She didn't understand his win-at-all-cost ideals then, Lani thought, a wry smile on her face. He seemed so self-assured, so mature. She didn't know that he was fine... as long as he won. Ken was riding high after winning three straight conference hurdles championships. But when he lost for the first time, in his senior year, he went into a fit of depression that never really disappeared. His brooding led to flair ups over the most insignificant things. Shaking her head wistfully, Lani remembered trying to bolster his confidence, willing to stand by him, even taking his

# Conquering Embrace 35

abuse. But nothing worked. She could still feel the pain of trying to console him only to have Ken snap at her, treating her like a meddlesome fly, like a non-person. His perspective on winning and losing was totally unrealistic.

When Lani started winning her collegiate tennis matches, things got worse. Ken seemed to resent her success. This hurt, too, but she chalked it up to his male ego and clung to the hope that once they were married, he would realize she wasn't competing with him, that all she cared about was being happy with him.

Lani zipped up her gear bag, hung it over her shoulder, and strode out of the locker room, down the cool, dark concrete corridor leading to the courts. Her thoughts of the past continued, falling into rhythm with the squeaking of her rubber-soled sneakers on the concrete floor.

When Ken broke their engagement with feeble excuses about the relationship cramping his training schedule, Lani was stunned. Afterwards, he put more distance between them, always in a rush, never having time to see her. The final blow came when Lani discovered he'd been dating the campus homecoming queen. The pretty, reserved young woman was a complete contrast to Lani. Where Lani was self-assured and competitive, the homecoming queen was demure, thoroughly adoring, and absolutely non-threatening. When Ken and she were married, Lani was numb with shock, realizing finally that Ken's fragile ego simply couldn't handle a strong-willed, competitive woman. He got what he needed, Lani thought. He was free to waste his life, pursuing dreams of sports glory, secure that when he came home, win or lose, he didn't have to worry about being bested by his wife. What a fool he was! And how naïve she had been not to see it all sooner.

Lani came out of the tunnel onto the court area and was engulfed in warm sunlight and a burst of brilliant color. The posh tennis club was a beehive of activity. While the players were going through their warm-ups, friends and fans were chatting in the stands. Nobody seemed to notice the hundred-degree heat.

The cacophony surrounding the tournament buzzed through the air and Lani quickly became caught up in the excitement of the competition. Her musings about Ken were replaced by her eagerness to play.

Lani found the tournament director and received her first pairing and court number from the A-players tournament roster. She recognized the name of the woman she'd be pitted against in the first match. Quickly glancing at her court, Lani saw a formidable redhead stripping off her warm-up suit, getting down to business. Just her luck, Lani thought, to be paired against the tournament's top female seed in the first match. If she could win this opening match, Lani speculated, then she'd be halfway home to winning the tournament. Lani stowed her bag and moved onto the court, stretching her legs, trying to get the juices flowing.

As the two women exchanged warm-up shots, Lani tried to block out all feelings for anything other than the here and now. She'd need all her concentration, she realized, as the spunky redhead returned her shots from both the forehand and backhand sides with ease.

After about five minutes the opponents completed their warm-ups and Lani jogged over to the players' bench, sat down and took a sip of cool water from the nearby water fountain. Lani noted she was already perspiring, and for the first time she was aware of the heat. Yesterday had been dry and breezy; today was much more humid and Lani scanned the sky overhead, seeing a smattering of clouds blown in from the ocean.

The referee signaled the start of the match and Lani took her spot behind the baseline, serving first. Composing herself, gazing around, she saw only about half a dozen people sitting in the small grandstand. Good! she thought. Less people meant less noise and distraction.

Gently rocking on her feet, she tossed the ball high with her left hand and with her right, whipped the head of the racket through the air in a smooth, fluid motion, smacking the ball with a resounding *pop!* The serve zipped in for a winner. Lani was on and she easily took the first game. Her energy level was high, her concentration fixed on the ball; and she moved with the sleek agility of a cougar. Her sure, classic strokes soon took their toll. Her fluid game of graceful power had the quick-footed redhead scampering futilely back and forth across the court trying to chase down Lani's well-placed shots. With growing confidence fueling her energy, Lani took the first set: 6 to 2.

Taking a brief rest on the bench between sets, Lani took another drink of water and ran a towel over her face and neck. Despite the relatively easy time she had in the first set, she was drenched in perspiration. The heat was nearly oppressive, Lani thought, as she flipped off her soaking sweatband and grabbed a fresh one from her bag. The sun was definitely going to be a factor, she believed, as she wiped off her racket handle and stood up to receive her opponent's opening serve of the second set.

The agile redhead served well but Lani won the game anyway. Lani was taking over where she had left off at the end of the first set, stroking good. But, as she prepared for her own serve, Lani began to dwell on the sun and the heat. For some reason, she was starting to feel just a bit more tired, a bit less quick. Her first serve hit the top of the net; her second did the same, and her game went downhill from there. The more she tried to concentrate and make her shots, the more it seemed she made errors. Before she knew it, the redhead was leading. Lani pushed harder only to become so frustrated she began to fear she'd lose the set and maybe the match. Lani had definitely lost the edge.

The opportunistic redhead was quick to seize the advantage, swinging the momentum of the match her way. Balls that she had been able to reach earlier, now had Lani running helter-skelter across the court, adding to her frustration while sapping her energy.

The redhead continued to peck away with her methodical spin-serve. As Lani lunged to return a wide shot, she heard a resounding *ping* and the ball seemed to die on her racket. Damn! She'd broken a string. Signaling "time" to the referee, Lani walked toward the bench, shaking her head.

The grandstand was nearly full by now and, as Lani bent to her bag to retrieve another racket, a tall figure, stretched out lazily on the upper row, caught her eye. It was hard to make out his face from beneath a rumpled baseball cap but there was definitely something familiar about him. When he broke into a broad grin and waved in her direction, Lani realized it was Bo. His lanky, well-defined limbs, clearly outlined beneath the fabric of a light gray suit, gave Lani an instant reminder of the uneasiness she'd felt the night before. Just what she needed! As if things weren't going bad enough already, now she had to deal with a major distraction. She was in no mood to return his smile and, after checking her new racket to make sure all the strings were intact, she begrudgingly acknowledged Bo's presence with a curt nod and strode back to the service line to resume play.

Now Lani felt as if she was in the spotlight, sure that Bo was judging her every move. This only made her play worse. The intrepid redhead served out the set, winning it: 6 to 4. Lani had started out like gangbusters but she was clearly at a disadvantage now and with Bo's presence looming over her from the grandstand she was becoming unglued.

Slumping back on the bench for another rest between sets, Lani refused to scan the grandstand for Bo. She merely sat back with a towel over her head trying to shake off the spell that had come upon her. She could just imagine him sitting here, smugly watching her lose, gloating with that superstar ego.

"Looks like she's got you on the run, Lani."

The words broke through Lani's thoughts like a gunshot. Whipping the towel off her head, she turned to see

## Conquering Embrace 39

Bo kneeling behind the bench, his arms resting lazily across the back, his eyes focused directly at her, a scant few inches from her own. The arrogant smugness she'd expected to find was nowhere on his smiling face.

"It's nothing I haven't been through before. I'll manage fine, thank you." Lani tried to sound unconcerned with her performance, but Bo picked up the note of tired exasperation in her voice. He continued to smile at her pleasantly, further unnerving her. "What are you doing here anyway? I didn't know you were a tennis fan," she said, straightening up and facing him.

"Oh, I'm a fan of a lot of things." He winked. "Actually, since you couldn't have lunch with me, I figured the next best thing would be to see you play."

"See me screw up, you mean," Lani countered, removing her second sweatband, as wet as the first.

"You're not doing so bad actually; you're just pressing a little too hard," he offered casually.

"Don't tell me you're an expert on tennis too?" Lani snipped sarcastically. But Bo seemed unperturbed as he stared at her with a disarming smile of understanding. She quickly regretted her remark. "I didn't mean that, Bo." Trying to change the subject, she said, "Aren't you dressed kind of fancy for a dumb little club tournament?" She smiled for the first time, gazing at his well-tailored silk suit.

"I guess so," he laughed, "but I'm leaving here to catch a flight to Pittsburgh. We play our opening game in a few days."

"Pittsburgh–San Diego, of course. The first big Monday night TV game." Lani remembered the talk she'd overheard at the office. "Well, good luck, Bo," she offered, as she stood up to start the third and final set. "Nice of you to drop by."

But before she could walk back to the court, Bo stood up and caught her arm. When Lani turned back to him, she was drawn to his eyes, scanning her features, probing deeply. She felt an electric charge jolt through her arm and she became aware of a droplet of perspiration gently sliding down her inner thigh.

She saw Bo's lips curve into a wide smile, easing the momentary tension. "Lani, I know this match is important to you, even if this is just a little club tournament, as you put it. I know what you're going through. Believe me, I've been there before. You've got the strokes to beat this gal; you've just lost a bit of confidence is all."

"I wish somebody would tell *her* that," Lani sighed realizing that Bo was trying to help.

"When I'm in the same spot, getting killed by a team I know the Lions can beat nine times out of ten, I get frustrated just like you are now. But over the years, I've learned a few things and, when I reach that point, I try to block out everything from my mind except myself and the ball. There's nothing else. Just me and the ball. Your body's a finely tuned instrument that, given the chance, can do everything you want. Let it make the shots and if you miss one or two don't make things worse by berating yourself. Forget about it and go on to the next shot. Just focus on the ball. Don't pay any attention to noises, the weather, or anything else. You'll see. Your body will do its thing and those shots will be zipping back across the net just like they did in the first set. Don't let the competition get to you. In fact, think of yourself as a machine that works better the tougher things get. You'll win easily, believe me." He continued to smile his encouragement, relaxing his grip on her arm.

Lani was unprepared for this unselfish offer of advice. It was obvious he was a pro, a veteran of competition. If anybody knew the key to turning her game around, perhaps Bo did. Staring into his hazel eyes, Lani felt her heart settle down and she breathed easier. "Thanks, Bo. I'll give it a try." She returned his smile and started to walk back to the service line.

"Lani..."

She cocked her head back to Bo and saw him take off his hat. He tossed it and she caught it.

## Conquering Embrace           41

"You need a hat; this sun's murder," he called, waving as he climbed back into the grandstand.

Lani put the hat on her head and took her place to receive serve, filled with a new determination.

Lani attacked the redhead's serve with ferocity. Her opponent took the game but Lani made the woman work hard for every point. And, just as Bo had suggested, Lani didn't dwell on her own missed shots; she didn't berate herself. With Bo's hat keeping the intense sun from broiling her brains, Lani focused solely on the ball. The crowd, which was beginning to get involved in the match, applauded more and more as the women extended themselves. But Lani's concentration was riveted to the ball and the cheering spectators became a muffled nonentity, safely delegated to some undefined locale in the background. She allowed herself only an occasional look in Bo's direction and, after they exchanged knowing glances, she returned her attention to the ball.

Lani's serve was once again smooth and accurate. It wasn't long before she had the redhead on the run. Even though this spunky woman was a top A-player, one of the best Lani had faced since college, Lani's confidence continued to build. Rocking on the balls of her feet, springing catlike for every shot, Lani enjoyed the competition with the fervor of an excited schoolgirl. Her dress was soaked with perspiration and beads of sweat flowed in rivulets down her arms and legs. Lani enjoyed every sensation.

Her nerves steady, her reflexes acute, Lani merely let her body go to work. Her performance was exhilarating. When the redhead nailed a groundstroke, Lani enjoyed it even more because it gave her body the opportunity to use every ounce of its ability to run down the shot and send it back with her own screaming shot. The *pop, pop, pop* of the ball hitting the rackets was the only sound she seemed to hear.

After an extended series of volleys at the net, Lani won the point and she and the redhead paused a moment to stare into each other's eyes, aware of the effort they were each putting out, acknowledging the great tennis they were playing.

The third and final set went down to a tiebreaker. Lani won it and beaming inside, smiling tiredly on the outside, Lani shook the redhead's hand at the net. Walking back to the bench, grabbing her towel, Lani looked up to see Bo grinning at her.

He came down from the grandstand and walked back to the clubhouse with her. She made no effort to resist when Bo casually slid his arm around her waist and joked with her about how well she played once she got over her jitters. As they approached the refreshment stand, Lani felt a new respect for Bo. Unlike Ken, Bo wasn't intimidated by a strong, competitive woman. He had no second thoughts about offering soothing words of reassurance, knowing full well that it just might be enough for her to win and, in a way, put her on equal footing as an athlete. This was definitely a plus in her book. This was a sign of maturity, a sign that he could go beyond the confines of athletics, without feeling insecure. The thought of working to make Bo a top advertising prospect came into her mind and Lani surmised that Bo probably had just what it took.

He bought them Cokes and they took seats at a white metal-and-glass patio table. Thankful for the shade provided by the large umbrella rising from the center of the table, Lani took a long cool drink, picked an ice cube out of the cup and ran it across her forehead.

"I really enjoyed that, Lani. You put on quite a show," Bo complimented casually.

"Thanks to you. It's amazing what can happen with just a few encouraging words. But when does a pro football player find the time to play tennis?" Lani asked as she wiped her towel across her forehead.

"I haven't played since...well since college, anyway. It's just that some things, like psyching out an opponent and knowing how to win, are common to all

# Conquering Embrace 43

sports." He punctuated the comment with an intimate stare.

Lani let the ice cube she was sucking fall slowly back into the cup. She realized he was staring at her glistening lips and, without taking her eyes from him, she wiped an errant trickle of water from the corner of her mouth. She got the impression that he was planning his next victory... over her.

"Do you always win, Bo?" Lani's voice was teasing, but she was curious to hear his answer.

"No, not always, but, if I want something bad enough, I usually find a way to get it." His tone was matter of fact but the smoldering, emerald hue in his eyes sent a clear message of desire.

Lani slowly turned to the action on a nearby court but her mind wouldn't focus on the match underway. Her thoughts were still on Bo. She found herself shifting back to his smiling face, to his sensuously curved lips. Could he possibly know how he was effecting her? He was probably as practiced handling women as he was in throwing a football Lani thought. He had to sense her growing uneasiness, *and* her awakening desire.

Lani tried to think of something intelligent to say to break the silence. Her eyes continued to search the rugged, sculpted features of his face when she suddenly realized there was something different about him. His hair was cut short, giving his masculine features a clean-cut, almost boyish look. "That's quite a crewcut you've got; it almost makes you look like a teenager," Lani joked as she bit into another ice cube.

Bo's eyebrows arched in amusement. He leaned back in his chair and ran a hand across his bristly, reddish-brown hair. "One of the trainers moonlights as a barber and usually gives me a trim at the beginning of the season. It's easier to keep neat and I find that it's a lot more comfortable inside a hot helmet. But don't worry, it'll grow back."

Lani started to laugh and had to suck hard on the ice

cube, making a loud slurping sound to keep it from falling out of her mouth. "I like it actually, it's kind of cute."

Bo leaned forward again. "Lani, I know we got off on the wrong foot last night and I'm sorry if I acted rude or inconsiderate."

Lani sobered quickly at his words. Her eyes turned to his, staring deeply into the green-brown pools beneath his shaggy brow.

"It's not often I meet someone like you. Sure, there are plenty of women hanging around, trying to get their hooks into a well-paid athlete, but they're so shallow and what they're after is so obvious. But you're... well, you're something special. I hope you don't hold my momentary indiscretion at the restaurant against me?" he asked, flashing the most charming smile. The way his eyes crinkled at the corners quickly dispelled any resentment she still felt over the incident at their dinner table last night.

"No harm done, I suppose. You're forgiven," Lani relented.

"Good. For a while there, I thought I might've ruined everything. I hope you're still agreeable to helping me out with my retirement plans."

Amused by his tact, and at ease with his unimposing manner, Lani feigned a stern, officious voice. "Well, Bo, I've given the matter some thought and, all things considered, it might be in the interest of my agency to reconsider your request, provided our research department can come up with the necessary data to indicate such a move could be in our mutual interest."

"What the heck does that mean?"

"It means, of course, I'd love to put you on the team." Lani laughed and Bo shook his head, grinning back his satisfaction.

"Wonderful. I knew you and I could see eye to eye. We'll make a great team, Lani, you'll see." Bo looked at his watch. "It's time I was pressing on, Lani. My

## Conquering Embrace  45

flight leaves in half an hour. Care to walk me back to my truck?"

"Sure, Bo. I've still got a few minutes until my next match." Lani stood up, letting him take her hand in his as they headed toward the parking lot.

They walked quietly across the open tarmac and Lani felt surprisingly comfortable next to Bo as he lightly gripped her hand. They quickly arrived at his truck and Bo suddenly halted and turned her toward him. "I have to go, Lani, but I want you to know I certainly enjoyed spending this time with you." His features softened and his eyes took on a liquid glimmer.

Lani's heart began to pound heavily as she stood close, looking up at him. He placed both hands on her waist and her eyes focused on his lips as they parted slightly.

Lani's thoughts were muddled and her spine began to tingle as Bo's eyes flashed emerald sparks of desire.

"Your hat, Bo," Lani murmured absently. She started to take it off, but Bo intercepted her hand and slowly guided her arm over his shoulder. He then encircled her slender waist and drew her toward him.

"Keep it," he breathed huskily.

Lani's gaze was riveted to his lips as they moved closer. With all her senses alert and her heart pounding wildly, she tilted her mouth up to meet his.

Closing her eyes she felt Bo press his lips against hers in a breathy, fiery kiss. His arms moved up and around her back, drawing her firmly against his entire muscled length, jolting her body with electric waves.

Lani responded, folding her arms around his neck, meeting his intense urgency with her own. His tongue probed gently against her soft, wet lips and she opened them obligingly, urging him on. She took his now demanding tongue, feeling it explore the soft inner lining of her mouth, caressing it with her own hot, moist tongue, while feverishly working her lips against his.

Her mind and body swirled as she nibbled lightly on

the tip of Bo's tongue, realizing that despite his expensively tailored silk suit, he was holding her soaking wet body firmly against him. His warmth radiated throughout her entire body and a throaty moan escaped from her parted lips.

Lani slowly began to remember that they were standing in the middle of a parking lot, acting as if they were the last people on earth. Only a scant few moments had passed but to Lani it could've been hours.

As if by mutual agreement, they slowly opened their eyes and their lips separated though they remained in each other's arms.

"I guess you'd better be on your way, Bo, or you'll miss your plane," Lani breathed, breaking the silence.

"I'm afraid so, Lani. But I'll call you when we get back in a couple of days." Bo relaxed his grip and Lani took a step back. "This is one time I'd just as soon miss the opening game."

"We can't have that now, can we? You've got to make a good showing so your fans will remember it when you're trying to convince them they need to buy more sherry... or underwear, right?" Lani laughed while opening his truck door for him.

"Yes m'am." Bo gave her hand a parting squeeze. Then he stepped into the cab and started the engine. "I'll be back Tuesday night, I'll give you a call then."

Lani nodded her reply and as he put the truck into gear she yelled, "Thanks for the hat, Bo."

He stuck his head out of the driver's window and yelled back at her, "You're welcome. Give 'em hell in the tournament, Lani."

Lani waved as the truck disappeared out of the driveway, moving toward the airport. She then turned and headed back toward the clubhouse. Spinning the cap around her index finger, she jogged back to the courts, eager to meet and beat her next opponent in the tournament.

# 4

WITH A NOTE of tired indifference, Lani dictated the end of a memo into the slim microphone in her hand. "In summation, while we feel that Mr. Liscomb shows excellent potential as a director, we have nothing in our current list of projects that would be appropriate for him at this time. Thank you for giving us the opportunity to view Mr. Liscomb's work. Should we have a change in our production schedule, we will give Mr. Liscomb further consideration. Yours truly, et cetera, et cetera." Lani switched off the miniature dictation recorder and pushed the eject button, popping out the small cassette tape. Sliding her high-backed office chair from her desk, she swiveled around toward the large picture window and stared out of her office toward the harbor in the distance.

Rubbing her fingers over her temples, Lani paused for a few moments, thankful that she'd finally cleared her desk of the piles of mundane chores. In the two days since she'd seen Bo at the tennis club, Lani had attacked the backlog of work piled high on her desk. But even though she'd managed to wade through all of it, her thoughts were continually drawn back to the virile quarterback. She could still feel the tingling warmth of his kiss during their embrace.

Getting out of the chair, Lani shook out the wrinkles from her mauve linen suit and reached for the coffee cup sitting on her desk. Peering back through the window, she met her reflection in the thick, smoked glass. Her tanned face, framed neatly by her soft-shouldered jacket and the white lace of her Victorian-collared blouse, mirrored her boredom. Lani ran her slim fingers through her hair, trying to clear the cobwebs that seemed to cover everything in her mind except her thoughts of Bo. Looking down at the street ten stories below, she stared at the people moving around, feeling apart from everything save the memory of Bo's kiss.

She took a sip from her cup and frowned at the taste of the acidic coffee. She put the cup back on her desk and slumped down on the settee in her office. Slipping off her shoes, she put her feet up on the wood and glass coffee table, scattering the few magazines piled on it. Perhaps her position was unladylike, but she wasn't paid to be ladylike and in the solitude of her office she couldn't care less. Flexing her toes and gazing at the neatly framed seascape etchings that decorated the walls, Lani sighed, wondering how she'd managed to get involved with an athlete again. Was she gullible enough to be coaxed by Bo's unbridled confidence? Or was it his magnetic charm? Whatever that indefinable quality was that he exuded, she'd certainly been snared by it. After what she'd felt about Ken and all he stood for, Lani was surprised to find herself back in the forbidden territory. But Bo certainly wasn't Ken. Lani understood that, even though they both pursued similar goals. She knit her brow in consternation. Maybe it was the way Bo carried himself off the field—like a winner. And he certainly wasn't

## Conquering Embrace 49

hung up about dealing with a strong, competitive woman. She had to take it slow, however, and not jump to conclusions. The best course was to simply take things as they happened. But what would happen the next time his probing eyes stared deeply at her, the next time his lips moved close to hers?

Lani's thoughts were interrupted by a knock on the door and the sudden appearance of her assistant, striding into the office with a large portfolio under one arm and a stack of scripts in the other.

"What is it, Joyce? Not more work I hope."

The bouncy young blond set the papers on the desk as Lani stretched and rose from the couch.

"'Fraid so, chief. These are the scripts for the toothpaste tasters, the coffee cranks, and the sherry slurpers."

"I suppose Charlie wants them all read post haste and discussed at this afternoon's meeting?" Lani sighed.

"That's what he said," replied Joyce with an understanding smile.

"What's that?" Lani asked glancing at the portfolio.

"Some of the artwork for the magazine ads that are going to the printer this week." Joyce spread open the wide folder revealing several paste-ups and glossy photographs.

"And here I am thinking I've made a little headway in the weekly pile of work," Lani reflected as she thumbed through the material with a perfunctory glance. One photo caught her eye. It was of Bo, smiling, holding a glass of sherry. It was a production still from the commercial they shot last Saturday. Lani held it up, noting the slick, smooth image of the equally smooth and slick quarterback. She returned it to the pile and spotted another photo of Bo, one she had not expected. The beaming quarterback in a locker room, wearing only an open tuxedo shirt and a pair of brightly colored men's bikini briefs. He appeared to be taking off the shirt and something about his smile indicated the underwear would be next.

"We don't handle any underwear accounts, do we?" Lani asked, still staring at the photo.

"That must be from the stuff Charlie was looking at earlier. He needed to check out whatever else we had in the files on Cornell. Charlie must've slipped it in with the others," Joyce surmised as Lani held up the photo for closer examination. "They certainly broke the mold after they built that one," Joyce cooed, looking over Lani's shoulder.

Lani studied the photo, impressed with Bo's well-defined physique. The photo made a simple statement, showing the product to it's best advantage. Bo's rugged good looks projected vividly and the more Lani stared at his image, the more she felt a nervous flutter build inside her. Whoever thought up that ad sure knew what they were doing, she mused. She doubted the ad would inspire many men to purchase the obviously male product on their own, but Joyce's gushing comment was evidence enough that if women thought the product was sexy, then men would undoubtedly want to emulate Bo.

"Joyce, what do you know about Bo Cornell?" Lani asked, trying to make her interest seem merely casual.

"Not much really... just the usual gossip."

"Well, c'mon girl. If he's going to be a regular with us, every little bit helps," Lani goaded, trying not to sound too anxious.

After a moment's pause, Joyce began, "My boyfriend, George, says Cornell's the number one target of sports groupies. How does *he* know, you're thinking, right? George practically lives and breathes by what he reads in the sports page so you've got to take what he says with a grain of salt. But, according to the press, Cornell has made a reputation as some kind of stud."

"Seems I've heard something like that myself," Lani agreed sardonically, recalling the incident with the waitress.

"George says that it's really a front, that Cornell's got people writing press releases making him seem like a sex

## Conquering Embrace    51

symbol. George told me that Cornell is really afraid of women, doesn't know how to handle 'em. But you know what it is? George is just jealous, like most of the guys he hangs around with at the bar, drinking beer and watching the football games every week."

The last remark struck a chord within Lani. Here's a successful athlete, soon to retire as one of the city's great stars and the women fall all over him, while the men sit around making jokes to hide their jealousy. Lani walked back to the window, crossed her arms and stroked her chin as the germ of an idea started to grow. She gazed across the expanse of city beneath her, realizing that here was a personality with a built-in fan club. And Bo's reputation was probably flourishing in other parts of the country as well. With the right approach, getting him just enough media exposure, making sure his occasionally reckless behavior didn't get in his way, Bo could be a hit.

Lani's phone buzzed and Joyce picked up the receiver, listened, and punched the conference call box on Lani's desk. Joyce mouthed the word "Charlie."

"Hello, Charlie, what can I do for you?" Lani called from across the room.

The box on her desk squawked the reply of the company president. "Lani, that commercial you shot Saturday is back from the lab and the editors have made a rough cut. I thought you might like to come by the conference room after lunch and take a look, okay?" the man replied lightly with a touch of a Boston accent.

"Sure thing, boss, I just might have something interesting to discuss with you, too," Lani replied.

"Well, take your time. The film won't be ready until three. Later..."

Looking at her watch, Lani realized she had a couple of hours to kill. "How about lunch, Joyce? There's a great Mexican restaurant over by Balboa Park."

"Sounds good, Lani, but I've got to wait for George. He's coming to pick me up and take me to the garage.

My car's on the fritz again. Want me to book you a reservation somewhere?"

"No, that's all right, maybe I'll head out to the Mexican place by myself. The park is right across the street. I'll get some takeout and find myself a nice shady spot," Lani replied, sorry that she couldn't use the time to ask Joyce what else her boyfriend had picked up from the sports page. Glancing at her watch again, she slipped on her shoes, picked up her shoulder bag and a couple of scripts.

"Lani, I also heard that Cornell may do a centerfold for that new women's playmate magazine," Joyce added.

"What!" Lani looked up incredulously. "You don't mean a nude centerfold?"

"Could be, least that's what I heard," Joyce replied. "If it's true, I'll grab us a couple of copies," Joyce added with a wink.

"Why that's insane, how could he? It would give him a reputation we'd never be able to promote," Lani said, half to herself.

Joyce picked up the photo from the underwear ad. "Oh, I don't know. Seems like the more I see of this one, the more I like. Know what I mean?" Joyce giggled.

"Oh, really, Joyce," Lani scolded, but Joyce's silly grin made it impossible for her to maintain her stern countenance and she broke into a broad grin of her own before heading out the door for the elevators. "See you later, girl, and try not to steam up the windows too much."

"Meeting's at three, don't forget," Joyce yelled after her.

"Right." Lani punched the button for the elevators and stepped through the yawning steel doors of the open car.

At the little tortilla factory that also doubled as a Mexican takeout stand, Lani bought a tostada and a Mexican fruit soda and strolled across the street to the pastoral elegance of Balboa Park. She found a nice spot, far enough away from the groups of other workers on their lunch breaks and the children scampering back and forth across the grass. It was a warm, clear day, with just a smattering of white, billowy clouds and a cooling breeze blowing in from the ocean. She leaned her head back and closed her eyes. She inhaled deeply, smelling the grass and flowers, while thinking of the meeting with Charlie. But the more she tried to relax the more her mind flooded with images of Bo's photograph.

She unwrapped the tostada and held the flat, fried tortilla in the palm of one hand, gazing at the lettuce, tomato, refried beans, cheese, and salsa piled high on top, trying to decide where to start. She bit down with a crunch and came away with a delicious mouthful. After a drink of the cold, pineapple soda, Lani thumbed through the scripts. But while her eyes roamed over the pages, her mind strayed once again to Bo. She glanced at her watch. Time seemed to pass at a tortoise's pace.

A soccer ball came whizzing past, followed by two grade schoolers, a boy and a girl. As the children kicked the ball back and forth, Lani realized that Bo and the team must be back in town and were probably already practicing for next week's game. She tossed the idea of driving out to the playing field around in her head as she swallowed the last of the tostada. Sure, why not? With finality, Lani stood up, tossed her litter into a nearby trash can and strode toward her car.

After a quick ten-minute drive across town Lani pulled her Mustang into a parking lot of a college athletic field. As she walked through a large gate, Lani was greeted by a small wooden sign proclaiming: *Sid Gillman Field, Practice Home of the San Diego Lions*. In the distance Lani heard a chorus of grunts, concussive smacks, and an occasional whistle.

She reached the field and leaned against a waist-high, chain-link fence, marveling at the fifty or sixty men going through an intense series of drills. Putting on her sunglasses, straining against the bright glare, Lani scanned the field looking for Bo.

In the center of the field, two squads were running plays, while a coach watched from the side, reading instructions from a clipboard. He gave the offensive team a play and Lani spotted Bo, quarterbacking the offense, the only man with a red jersey. The rest of the team wore blue.

"Cornell!" the red-faced coach barked. "How about if you execute a pump fake toward the tight end, then count to two and throw that sucker for all you're worth."

Bo nodded and then huddled briefly with the rest of the players on his squad. When Lani first met Bo at the sound stage, she'd considered him tall, well-proportioned, trim, yet muscular. Now she was surprised to see him nearly dwarfed by the hulking giants that were his offensive line.

After a sharp clap of hands, the group broke the huddle and Bo jauntily took his place behind the center. With clipped precision, Bo barked out a series of numbers and the center hiked the ball. Lani shuddered as the men on both sides of the line exploded toward each other. Bo danced back and assumed his throwing position as the defenders beat their way toward him. Even though these giants were pawing desperately to get him, Bo deftly followed the coach's instructions, began the fake pump motion and then, cranking up his arm, he launched a perfect high and deep spiral. Lani followed the trajectory of the ball. It seemed to float. Then, as it angled down, a fleet-footed deer of a receiver glided underneath it, sixty yards downfield, and gathered it into his arms like a ripe plum. The defending player futilely grasped at air as the receiver sprinted toward the end zone.

Lani saw Bo standing back at the other end of the field staring at the action with a look of nonchalant satisfaction. After a few moments discussion with the coach, Bo started away from the group, removed his helmet and

## Conquering Embrace 55

headed off the field. He caught Lani's gaze and, after a slight pause, he broke into a wide grin and jogged over toward her.

"You wouldn't be here to visit me by any chance would you, Lani?" Bo smiled innocently, his hazel eyes flashing with delight.

"Well, since you mention it," she teased, "I was in the neighborhood with some time to kill. Just thought I'd see how you make your living when you're not in front of a camera."

Bo leaned over the little fence from the other side and placed a light kiss on her lips. The feel of his warm, soft lips on hers sent shivers up and down her spine. He pulled back and slid his eyes over her, obviously enjoying the diversion she provided. Perspiration trickled from his tousled, close-cropped hair. He wiped it off his forehead with the back of his hand. "I was going to call you tonight, but I'm glad you beat me to it. Sorry about my appearance," he continued, wiping off more sweat. "Those big lugs aren't supposed to hit me too much in practice but they get a real kick out of rolling me around in the dirt any time they get the chance." He broke into a hearty laugh. "'Course, those boys are groomed to hate quarterbacks, no matter if he's on the same team. So how did you do in the tournament?"

"I won, thanks to you," she answered, moving her liquid blue eyes over Bo's striking features. Standing next to her in full pads, Bo seemed to loom over her and Lani felt her palms moisten and her heart beat faster.

"Don't give me the credit, Lani. All I did was give you a little encouragement. You and that magnificent body of yours did the rest."

Lani felt her cheeks flush.

"I'm glad you won though. If you're anything like me, you'd be grumpy for days afterwards if you had lost."

Lani smiled, "Judging by your mood now, I'd say you won the Pittsburgh game."

"Yeah... I guess you don't read the sports page much."

"I'm going to start. I've heard there're some very interesting stories there," she answered, thinking of the tidbits Joyce's boyfriend picked up. "Say, won't your coach jump on you for taking it easy?" Lani asked as she saw the other players still hard at it, running through their drills.

Bo gave her a sly grin. "Naw, I've got my own schedule, practice whenever I want. That's one of the little benefits of stardom," he boasted.

"Cornell, get a move on. The trainer doesn't have all day," a nattily dressed coach ordered from the distance and Bo looked sheepishly back to Lani.

"Of course, sometimes everybody's got to play by the rules." He shrugged. "I've got to get a little whirlpool therapy. Care to walk over with me?"

"All right," Lani replied, removing her sunglasses and falling into step with Bo as he headed toward the nearby gym. For the first time, Lani noted a slight limp in Bo's gait as his spiked football shoes scraped against the concrete walkway.

"Bo, you're hurt..." Lani tried to mask the concern in her voice.

"Just a sprain, nothing serious. I guess those Pittsburgh players were a little hungry Monday night. They must have resented the two touchdown passes I tossed against them last year." He winked at her, but Lani knew how brutal pro football could be. Bo must have noted the concern on her face, because he smiled at her and said, "Don't concern yourself, Lani, really. Little nickel-and-dime injuries happen all the time. If I thought there was any real danger of serious injury I would have quit a long time ago." He took Lani's hand and strolled into the gym.

They stepped into a small, well-lit room filled with several padded tables, various exercise equipment, and three large, stainless steel tubs.

Lani heard several sharp taps against one of the tubs

## Conquering Embrace 57

and she turned to see a rumpled baseball cap pop up. It was followed by the head of an elderly, craggy-faced man with a Sherlock Holmes style pipe stuck between his lips.

"Hiya, Bo, I think I finally got this tub working," he said and turned on a spigot. The tub began filling with water.

"Wally," Bo answered, "I'd like you to meet a very special friend of mine, Leilani Richards."

"Pleased to meet you, m'am. Say, you're not one of those female sports reporters by any chance?"

The question surprised Lani. "No, I'm in advertising, why?"

"Oh, don't get me wrong, Miss Richards, I just heard from some of the guys in the other clubs that they're having a heck of a time keeping those women reporters out of the locker rooms. Some of the fellas don't mind, but I like to think of the locker room as a man's territory. I mean where can a guy go for, well, for sanctuary, if not a locker room. Next thing you know, lady reporters will be in the showers with the guys, asking questions, taking the guys' minds off the games, if you know what I mean... No offense of course," he relented, taking off his cap and scratching his head.

"I'm afraid Wally's from the old school," Bo said laughing, "before helmets and manners. But he's the best tape man around."

"That's okay." Lani smiled at Wally. "I can understand a man needing his sanctuary," she offered patting his shoulder affectionately.

By now the tub was full. Wally flipped on a switch and the water began to swirl furiously. He grabbed a small, alarm clock-type timer and set it. "I'd say you need about twenty minutes, Bo. Hop up on the table here for a second and let me look at your knee."

Bo did as Wally asked and removed his jersey and shoulder pads while Wally pulled his pants leg up past his knee. The trainer unwrapped a long, elastic bandage and Lani stared at the ugly black and blue bruises that seemed to cover Bo's entire knee area. She looked up at Bo's face.

He smiled back at her reassuringly.

"It looks worse than it is, just a bruise, right Wally?"

Wally ignored the question. "Has this been stiffening up overnight?"

"Not really," Bo answered, still smiling at Lani.

Wally gently fingered the bruised knee and then stood back. "You'll probably survive. C'mon, get in the tub."

Bo hopped off the table. A loud chorus of voices accompanied by feet echoing on the concrete floor, suddenly filled the air.

"'Fraid I'll have to ask you to leave, Miss Richards," Wally said. "Rest of the team is coming..."

"Oh, come on, Wally, don't be such a prude," Bo teased. "When's the last time we had such a beautiful addition to our stinky training room?" Bo unfastened his belt and was about to pull down his pants when the voices grew louder, announcing the arrival of the other players. The prospect of being the only woman in a gym filled with sweaty, bulging football players didn't sit well with Lani and she glanced at her watch.

"It's all right, I've got to be heading back to the office anyway."

"Wally, give us a minute will you?" Bo asked. "And keep those gorillas out of here, okay?"

Wally exhaled loudly, shaking his head. "Sure, Bo, but just a minute." He turned to Lani and tipped his cap. "A pleasure meeting you, Miss Richards," he said before walking out and closing the door behind him.

Bo stared at Lani and then moved close. He'd removed his half T-shirt and stood bare-chested. His well-defined torso was covered in wisps of dark brown hair, swirling around his sculpted pectoral muscles, trailing in a line down past his navel. His musky scent grazed Lani's nostrils.

## Conquering Embrace      59

"I'm really glad you came by, Lani," he began, his voice growing husky.

"I'm glad I did, too. I've never seen a pro football team practice before," Lani answered, finding herself drawn closer by his smoldering hazel stare.

"I've never met anyone like you, Lani. I've been thinking about you ever since the commercial. I thought you were prim and straightlaced at first, but you sure set me right. I like a confident woman, someone who knows what she wants and goes out and gets it. I could sense your intensity on the tennis court the other day. I knew how badly you wanted to win. I like that, Lani." Bo's eyes became heavy with desire.

Tilting her head upward, Lani looked deep into his eyes and felt her insides melting. Her pulse raced. "I don't always know what I want, Bo, but when I do..."

Bo placed his hands on Lani's shoulders and drew her against his chest. Closing her eyes, she offered her slightly parted lips in expectation.

"Romeo strikes again," somebody cackled, halting their movements. Lani opened her eyes and turned toward the door to see several faces peering in, framed by the doorway. They all broke into resounding laughter.

Bo released Lani and turned toward the players, hands on hips, annoyed but smiling nevertheless. "What's the matter with you guys? Where'd you learn your manners, in the zoo?"

"Sorry, guv," a slim, tall black player offered with mock sincerity. "We didn't realize you were in conference." He laughed and the others joined in before they all filed away from the doorway.

Bo shrugged helplessly and Lani smiled back at him. "I'd better be going, anyway." Lani leaned up to graze his cheek with a quick kiss. "Thanks for the tour," she said as she waved and started out the door.

"Lani, I want to see you again."

She turned back to him and stared at Bo's smiling

features, white teeth gleaming from behind his sweaty, dirt-streaked face.

"Lunch? Dinner? Anything you say," Bo coaxed.

A couple of the players returned and fidgeted around the doorway, anxious to use the whirlpool tubs. Lani felt uncomfortable answering Bo while they were waiting. "Okay, Bo. We'll talk later. 'Bye," she said, nodding and walking off. After a few steps she turned back and saw Bo grab a nearby towel and throw it at the grinning face of one of the teasing players.

Lani drove back to her office with her head in a swirl. Bo was as alluring as any man she could imagine. He was handsome, confident, and, unlike Ken, he wasn't threatened by a strong-willed, competitive woman. She swung the convertible toward downtown and tuned in the radio. Ironically, she punched a preselected station just as they were beginning the sports report. The announcer gave a rundown on scores and mentioned Bo's outstanding performance in the Pittsburgh game.

There was no doubt that, on the field at least, Bo was a star. Professionally she could do quite well with him, but the image of his badly bruised knee flashed in front of her and Lani's career objectives were quickly dispelled by her concern over Bo's injuries. She was no stranger to the rigors of athletics and despite Bo's denials, Lani knew that his knee probably hurt like hell.

Was he simply trying to conform to the traditional masculine role, never admitting pain, afraid to show weakness in front of a woman? Ken had been like that, Lani mused. He refused to take her into his confidence, refused to acknowledge her as a person who understood and cared. Could Bo possibly be the same way: Would he, in the end, prove to be the same immature little boy, unwilling to acknowledge the value of a woman at his side?

Lani gripped the wheel tightly until the strain made her hands cramp. She relaxed and the cramps eased and disappeared. Whatever her doubts about Bo, Lani realized that nothing could match the thrill of his kisses. Running her tongue across her lips, she could still taste the salt from his cheek. She knew that the more she was with him the less she'd be able to resist his power, to deny the wave of desire he stirred within her.

Lani pulled the Mustang into the underground parking lot beneath her office building, unsure of where things would lead with Bo but wanting to find out.

Her watch said three o'clock on the dot. As she headed upstairs to the conference room, her mind raced on. How sincere was Bo when he said she was all he thought about? How could she work with him in a professional capacity when her knees weakened and her spine tingled every time he looked at her with his flashing hazel eyes. She didn't know... but she knew she had to find out.

# 5

LANI SWUNG OPEN the large mahogany door and stepped into the conference room. Charles and his assistant, Jeffrey, were already seated at one end of the immense rectangular table.

"Lani, come on over and look at these," Charles said, indicating an open file folder in front of them. The preppy executive and his equally preppy assistant were evidently enjoying the various photographs they had spread before them.

She walked up to them and noted the same photos that were in the file Joyce had brought her before lunch. "I've already seen those, chief," Lani acknowledged, as she peered over Charles' shoulder.

"Jeff and I were thinking that Cornell just may be the new face we've been looking for for some of the slow accounts we've been stuck with," Charles said, as he leaned back in his leather chair and loosened his silk tie.

"Look at this, Lani," Jeffrey suggested, holding out a sheet of paper filled with numbers. "These are the sales figures on the number of men's bikini briefs sold before and after Cornell's commercial."

Lani held up the paper and perused the numbers. "I'd say that Mr. Cornell didn't hurt sales any," she replied, unslinging her shoulder bag and taking a seat next to them.

"Hurt them, are you kidding? Sales went up nearly forty percent since they aired his commercial," the slim assistant offered in response.

Lani continued to peruse the fact sheet and then handed it back to Jeffrey. "I don't see a breakdown on the number of pairs purchased by women, before and after the ad. That's where the real story is. How many women responded to the ad, buying them for their husbands, boyfriends, whatever, that makes the real difference. After all, the ad is tailored to appeal to women."

"That's my gal, er, woman...thinking all the time," Charles interjected, while picking at a piece of lint on his tweed sport coat.

"Does that mean you're finally going to give me that raise we both know is long overdue?" Lani teased.

"Hold on, now. Don't let a little compliment go to your head. I was just about to make a note for Jeffrey to run down those very same figures."

"Sure you were, chief," Lani sighed. "Anyway, you say the film's ready?"

"Right." Charles leaned over and grabbed the nearby phone on the table. He signaled the projectionist in the booth behind them that they were ready. The lights dimmed and a beam of light shot across the room hitting the screen that was previously hidden behind the wall. The scratchy, preliminary sound track noise came from large, concealed speakers.

As the film rolled through, Lani couldn't help being impressed by the smooth, natural way Bo came across. The quick, easygoing charm that emanated from him on

## Conquering Embrace 65

the sound stage, prevailed in the film as well. He seemed the perfect gentleman, thoroughly knowledgeable about the product, while exuding just a hint of virility, enough to imply that it was all right for a real man to enjoy an elegant drink like sherry. With a small amount of re-editing, and a polished sound track, the commercial would be super. Bo's expert work made Lani look good and it would undoubtedly appeal to the sponsor. The end of the film flapped through the projector and the lights in the conference room brightened.

Charles beamed his compliments to Lani for a job well done. "Excellent, Lani, just perfect. I don't know how you handled him but you sure did it right."

"It wasn't so tough," Lani replied. "A piece of cake really."

"Maybe it was the subject matter," Jeffrey interjected. "I heard that during the filming of the underwear commercial, he wouldn't keep a straight face. Seems that everytime he opened his shirt he'd wink at the girls on the set, or flex, or pull some other stunt that had everyone busting up take after take. They must've shot the darn thing fifty times..."

Lani looked again at the glossy photo from the underwear shoot and noted Bo's almost smirking grin. Whatever he did on the set probably caused the director to tear his hair out but, judging from the production still, that subtle curve in his lips was just the ticket for a successful ad campaign. Even when he was joking around it seemed that Bo had everything going his way.

"I understand you and Cornell get on quite well, Lani," Charles stated suggestively.

"Where did you hear that?" Lani replied, casting a suspicious eye at Jeffrey who sat next to her wearing a sheepish grin.

"I have my sources, but that's not important. What *is* important is that Cornell could be a real asset to our agency. He's got a lot of fans in the San Diego area as well as in the rest of the country. Now Jeffrey's already done some preliminary research and we know that Cornell isn't represented by an agent yet. We can deal with him directly. We've got several accounts that would be just perfect for him."

"You're not suggesting I corral him for the slow accounts you mentioned earlier?" Lani interrupted.

"That was just a thought. Judging from the film we saw, I'd say we can put him to better use than that. So what I'm suggesting is that you work on him. You've got the inside track, my dear. See if you can get him to commit to some of our projects."

"You're sure that's what you want, chief?" Lani asked, reflecting on her current situation with Bo and her emotional involvement. "I mean he's sort of the independent type and with football in full swing, I'm not sure how much time he can give us."

"Don't worry about that, Lani, leave it to me. Those jocks are all alike, get 'em in front of a camera and they forget about football, their wives, anything if it means they can be a star. What I'd like you to do is sell our company to him, show him how it's to his advantage to have us handle his imagemaking. Think you can handle that?"

"I guess so," Lani replied, knowing full well that Bo was eager for their company to court him as a media star. What she didn't know was how her own emotional involvement would interfere with her work. "If that's all, chief, I'll head back to my office and get on it."

Back in her office, Lani thumbed through her desktop phone directory and found Bo's number. As she dialed, questions poured through her mind. What would she say to Bo, how would she handle her job when her mind was a swirl of confused emotions? Bo was like a stone cast into her formerly calm waters.

She heard the phone ring, four, five times before someone picked it up.

"Hello?" Bo's voice drifted through the receiver.

## Conquering Embrace

"Hi, Bo, it's me, Lani."

"Lani, wonderful, how about dinner?"

Lani was caught off guard as he took the words right out of her mouth. "That sounds nice, Bo. But you should know I called for business."

"So we'll discuss business... among other things." Bo laughed. "How about we get together in about... how about now?"

Lani glanced at her watch and saw that it was only a few minutes after four. "It's a bit early for dinner, Bo."

"Nonsense, I like to eat at sunset, overlooking the ocean, so come on."

"Well... sure, early or late is fine with me," Lani finally agreed, while trying to think of a restaurant where they could meet. But he beat her to it again.

"I'll give you directions," Bo continued, his voice as eager as ever.

Lani listened and wrote down Bo's directions before realizing this restaurant he was suggesting was out of the way from any place she'd eaten in San Diego before. "This sounds like some kind of mysterious restaurant, Bo, what do you call it?"

"My place!" Bo replied in amusement. "You can't miss it. See you as soon as you get here and dress casual."

Lani hadn't expected this and she wondered if she should refuse to have dinner alone with him at his home. But, before she could reply, Bo made the decision for her.

"I'm really glad you called, Lani. It'll be a wonderful evening. You'll see, 'bye." He hung up and Lani held the receiver to her ear for a moment longer, nonplussed over her easy submission to Bo's suggestion. She hung up finally, realizing that during the events of the past few days, she'd been every bit as suggestive as he had been. It's now or never, girl, she told herself. If there was ever a time to answer the pounding of her heart and the nervous flutter in her stomach, this was it.

The Mustang purred around the winding road that

stretched along Point Loma's rugged coast. The sun was low in the sky and, as the nimble roadster tooled past the spectacular Sunset Cliffs, Lani marveled at the pink, orange, and purple hues that glinted off the ocean. Lani wasn't sure what Bo had meant when he told her to dress casually, but she made a quick stop at her apartment before heading toward his home. She stole a quick glance in the mirror, making sure the ocean breeze hadn't marred her carefully applied, understated makeup. She ran the tip of her tongue across her lips making the soft-toned lipstick glisten, showing her full lips to their best advantage. Little silver fans hung from her earlobes. Gray corduroy slacks and a pink knit polo shirt completed her outfit. Her hand tooled, Mexican leather sandals should do for just about anything, she surmised.

Lani checked the directions on the sheet of paper in her hand and, as the road took a steep incline upward, she saw a house perched high on a bluff, with the rugged Sunset Cliffs stretching perilously downward.

Lani pulled the Mustang into a circular driveway and stared at the modern home in front of her. Dark-grained wood beams and smoked glass dominated the front of the house. Stepping across the immaculately landscaped front yard, Lani reached the large front door and rang a little brass ship's bell hanging next to the doorway. A muffled bark sounded in response and the door swung open. There was Bo, leaning against the doorjamb, wearing an expansive smile. Beside him was King, panting and wagging his tail in greeting. Bo evidently meant it when he said casual because he stood barefoot, wearing faded, salty jeans and a tight-fitting, well-worn T-shirt.

"Welcome to my humble abode, Lani. Please come in," he offered holding out a hand and leading her inside.

Lani felt as if she'd stepped into Bo's well-appointed lair. "I'd hardly call this humble," she said with a sweep of her hand. "This is really beautiful, Bo."

"Thank you, but most of the credit should go to my architect, he managed to get this place anchored on this cliff, and it wasn't easy. You want the grand tour?" he asked warmly, still holding her hand.

"Of course, lead the way."

They stepped past the tile floored entry way into the main house and Lani realized the house wasn't nearly as large as it seemed from the outside. Bo's cozy living room featured a small, stone fireplace, wood floor, and several tasteful carpets. Otherwise, the furnishings were simple, understated. They suggested a bachelor's home but without any of the ultra-masculine touches that grow boring so quickly.

King padded after them into the small but efficient kitchen. It was obvious from the spread of professional chef's cookware, cutlery, and the layout of the counters, that Bo took pride in his ability as a cook. To her surprise, Bo led her to another room, paneled in rich, dark wood. The walls were lined with bookcases filled with an array of novels—many of them classics—technical manuals, and several video components. On one wall was a large TV projection screen. This was obviously his library and media room.

Walls in the rest of the house featured various prints and paintings with athletic themes. They weren't the usual tacky sports posters. One oil painting, different from all the rest of the artworks, portrayed a football player walking from the field, evidently after a game. His uniform was filthy, his face a study in pain, sweat, and dirt. A strip of tape hung raggedly from his wrist. All around the player the picture was filled with jubilation—fans cheering, flags waving, a scoreboard indicating the score—yet this lone player, oblivious to the celebration around him, wore the pained expression of a gladiator, victorious but emotionally removed from the victory. His face was a study in pathos.

"I'm impressed, Bo. I wouldn't have guessed a sports painting could be so intimate," Lani offered, sharing her feeling for the work.

"That's one of my favorites; I'm glad you like it."

"The rest of your home is impressive, too. It's... well, it's not something I'd expect from a bachelor."

"You mean from a bachelor jock, don't you?" He laughed, reading her thoughts perfectly.

"I guess so," she replied. She took a panoramic gaze, noting the high loft ceilings, thick exposed beams, and tall picture windows. Everything worked together, taking full advantage of the magnificent ocean view, equally accessible from the front or the back of the house. The setting sun was framed perfectly in the tall living room window and rays of orange light sprayed across the room.

"This is my favorite part of the day," Bo said. "You want to watch the sunset from the cliffs?"

"Okay," Lani replied.

Bo slipped on a pair of sneakers, took her hand, and guided her out a sliding door, across a red tiled patio, and down the precarious cliffs. As they walked gingerly over the odd shaped rocks, King scampered in front of them, choosing his own path, stopping occasionally to sniff out sand crabs.

"It looks dangerous, Bo," Lani said as she gazed down the jagged cliffs and saw the surf crashing against the rocks below. A few errant drops of spray drifted upward. Lani felt the cool ocean mist against her cheeks and smelled the salty aroma of seaweed. Overhead, gulls squawked gliding smoothly past them.

"It is," Bo acknowledged, "but if we're careful, we can climb down to a little niche I found that's fairly dry. You game?"

Lani was reluctant to venture down the jagged rocks but Bo's reassuring tone coaxed her anyway. With Bo leading the way, they clambered down the rugged cliff face, stopping occasionally to stare into teeming tide pools. Near the bottom Bo pointed to a sandy patch between the huge boulders. The low, orange sun lit the little niche like a bright oasis.

They sat on the warm sand and gazed seaward, protected from the spray flying around them.

## Conquering Embrace 71

Lani leaned back against Bo's chest, feeling snug and content until a loud bark suddenly pierced through their solitude. Lani jerked reflexively and Bo tightened his arms around her protectively. But when he laughed in amusement, Lani regained her composure and followed his eyes until she saw a mother seal and pup, disturbed from their sleep on a nearby rock. The seals slid noisily into the ocean and Lani returned her gaze to Bo. His smile faded and his lips softened. She felt his hot breath against her face. Then Bo slid a hand to the small of her back and drew Lani closer. Her breasts pressed firmly against his muscular chest, insulating her against the ocean air with a warmth that radiated throughout her entire body. Lani tilted her moistened lips to meet his. The setting sun's orange hue glinted magically off of Bo's eyes just before he closed them and gave Lani a soft but passionate kiss.

She felt an electric jolt shoot through her as Bo gently pushed his tongue between her yielding lips. She caressed his tongue with her own and squeezed herself tightly against him, swirling in a tide of desire, fully aroused by the delicious sensations. The surf surged and pounded below and, despite their well-chosen haven, a deluge of water cascaded over the rocks, showering them both in foamy spray.

Lani pulled back from the kiss and saw Bo's smiling face dripping wet.

"Tide's coming in," he said, as he stood and pulled her to her feet. "We'd better head back to the house. Besides, climbing these rocks in the dark isn't too wise."

Trying to brush the sand from her soaking clothes, Lani preceded him as they made their way back up the cliff. As if on cue, King met them at the top.

Bo kicked off his shoes before entering the house and Lani followed suit, stepping barefoot after him.

Turning toward her, Bo said, "We should probably get out of these wet clothes."

The suggestion sent giddiness rushing through Lani

and her pounding heart directed her response. "I suppose you're right..."

"I can throw these in the wash and there're plenty of large towels to wrap up in." Bo continued, his voice growing husky, his eyes flashing a message of desire. "I could make a fire..."

Lani reached up and gently placed her finger against his lips, silencing his words for more urgent matters. Bo suddenly reached for her and nimbly lifted her into his arms, carrying her off like an expectant bridegroom.

Lani snuggled her face against Bo's tanned cheek, holding him close with her arms around his neck. Running her lips across his face, she felt the alternating smoothness of his skin and the slightly rough texture of his beard. She enjoyed the sensation, continuing to brush her lips up and down his cheeks.

Bo carried her into his spacious master bedroom and gently placed her down on the king-sized bed. The overhead skylights and floor-to-ceiling windows bathed them in the last of the sun's light. As Lani eased back into the billowy down comforter, she looked up at Bo, focusing on the burning desire in his eyes.

Bo started to remove his shirt but Lani leaned up from the bed and stopped him. "Let me do it," she breathed hotly.

His intense stare softened and Bo gently lay down on the bed beside her.

Lani's hands were shaking, but desire drove her onward. With Bo laying on his back, his hands folded behind his head, he became a passive offering, served up for Lani to use as she wished. She ran her hands under his shirt and her fingers tingled as they grazed over the wisps of coarse hair that spread across his chest. Lani gently lifted Bo's T-shirt and roamed her eyes over the delineated muscles of his torso. As she had seen when he stood next to her bare-chested in the training room, Bo's athletic body had the finely tuned sleekness of a gazelle. She placed her lips on his flat, hard stomach

# Conquering Embrace

and drew lazy circles around his navel with her tongue. She began to kiss her way upward, across his pectorals, drawing his shirt over his head and off. Lani lightly tongued Bo's nipples and he groaned, unable to restrain his rising passion any longer.

"Now it's my turn," he murmured, rolling Lani over onto her back. She closed her eyes and ran her fingers through his short, bushy hair, grasping his head and drawing his lips down to hers.

As she drank in his kisses, Lani felt Bo reach under her polo shirt. Drawing his lips away, he made a quick, deft movement and pulled the shirt over her head, exposing her fully to his smoldering eyes. He settled beside her again, kissing her deeply. But, despite his urgency, Bo's hands were gentle as he moved them lightly over the swells of her full, dark breasts. His fingers began to draw circles around her nipples and Lani felt them growing hard under his touch. He ran his lips down her throat, over her breasts and took a nipple into his mouth.

Bo's mouth was a hot flame against her naked flesh and Lani groaned with pleasure. "Oh, yes, Bo, yes." The words escaped her lips as she reached down his back and ran her hand across the swell of his firm backside.

Bo drew his head back and Lani looked into his eyes as they scanned her in wanton appraisal. "You're beautiful, truly beautiful, my love," he proclaimed, his voice thick with desire.

They quickly shed the rest of their clothing and lay nude, facing each other on their sides. He ran a hand over her slender throat, over her shoulder, across her breasts, over her slim waist, and down her curving hips.

Lani repeated his actions, barely able to maintain her calm as her blood raced through her veins, her flesh hot and alive.

They flowed against one another and Lani felt Bo's muscled thighs press against hers. He reached a hand across the curving flair of her hips and drew her even closer to him.

Lani responded with feverish kisses, over his lips, his throat, biting his earlobe tenderly and he answered, gripping her waist and hips, pressing his tongue deep into her mouth, parting her thighs with his own. Lani felt his demanding masculine strength against her.

"I want you, Lani. I must have you," Bo murmured as he kissed the corner of her mouth, her eyelids, her breasts.

Bo's husky demands added fire to Lani's own passion and she moaned with pleasure. "Yes, Bo, I want you, too." She twisted her hands through his hair, totally under the spell of his caresses. Her arms tightened possessively around him. Her slender fingers stroked the taut muscles of his back, his thighs, over the sculpted curves of his hips. She arched her hips upward and met the heated, hard perfection that demanded her love. She could feel the surge of power that she was drawing from this magnificent man as he took complete and final possession of her.

They moved slowly, two athletes' bodies working in unison, discovering a common rhythm. She could feel Bo's heart beating against her breasts, like an ember catching flame, as his passion mounted. She'd never experienced this kind of lovemaking before and Lani met his fevered movements with her own, surrendering herself completely. Their heavy breathing quickened, coming in short gasps. His musky scent fired her passion even hotter and with her senses raging Lani felt her universe dissolving around her. The heated desire in her loins rose until she reached the peak of her ecstasy and her cry of passion was met by Bo's.

When Lani surfaced, it seemed as if hours had passed. She opened her eyes to see Bo smiling gently, his eyes warm, liquid pools. She stretched like a cat and reached a caressing hand to his cheek, purring her contentment. Still nude, he rose from the bed and lit a small, brass oil lamp. The subdued glimmer of the primitive lamp softly highlighted his body. She stared in appreciation at his

## Conquering Embrace 75

classic features, at her sculpted Greek Adonis. He moved back to the bed and, lifting the comforter for her, joined her under the covers.

"You hungry, darling?" Bo asked as he brushed a few strands of her dark hair from her brow.

"Mmm, yes, Bo, for you..." she cooed languidly.

Bo's eyes flashed a wicked gleam. "I feel the same way too, Lani," he said softly, sliding his body against her.

Lani snuggled close, resting her head in the crook of his arm, throwing an arm across his expansive chest, toying with the swirl of furry hair around one of his nipples.

Lani's heart beat a regular rhythm. She was totally relaxed yet sensitive to every subtle nuance of their bodies. She knew Bo must be feeling the same.

"Lani, I knew from the first moment I laid eyes on you it could be like this."

Lani twisted her head upward and pressed her lips lightly against his, running the tip of her tongue gently across his lower lip. Then, looking up from under her lowered lashes, she felt the giddy urge to tease him. "Really, Bo, the very *first* moment you saw me?" she asked coyly.

Bo's eyes, softened from their lovemaking, crinkled in amusement. "Well, maybe not the *first* moment. You were a bit domineering."

"Domineering?" she retorted, furrowing her brow, feigning displeasure at the remark.

"Yeah, you've got to admit, you did come off pretty much like the tough boss," he teased lazily while lightly tracing the outline of her mouth with his forefinger.

She stiffened. "Why, Bo Cornell, if you had seen the way you looked, waltzing onto the set, like...like some kind of crazy mountain man...late, loud, and arrogant..."

Bo silenced her with another kiss. "You're beautiful Lani," he added as he drew back. "Even though things were a little shaky at first, I could tell you were something special."

"Well..." she let the doubtful syllable drag out, watching the confidence in his features begin to flicker and fade. She suppressed the urge to giggle. "I will admit I was a little intrigued with you, Bo..."

Bo raised his eyebrows skeptically at her aloof tone.

The irrepressible urge to giggle rose in Lani's throat. She began to nibble on his earlobe. "Now that you've brought it up, Bo, I guess I am a bit hungry."

Bo threw back his head and laughed. But, after a moment, he leveled his gaze at Lani and she saw his nostrils flair slightly. His eyes darkened, as if he were a wild animal in search of game.

"These interludes really do work up an appetite," she breathed seductively.

Bo's lips curled slightly and Lani ran her slender fingers along the side of his lean torso, feeling his muscles ripple beneath her touch. A shiver of goosebumps coursed down her back and Lani felt her nipples harden again, rising into dark peaks.

Bo's eyes smoldered anew and he slid the comforter slowly from her, drinking in her exposed glory.

"I covet your beautiful body, Lani. I'm hungry for you, now," he said breathily.

Stirred by his rising desire, Lani's heart thumped harder in her chest. Her breathing deepened and her breasts began to rise and fall invitingly toward Bo. "You sound like some kind of savage animal," Lani breathed through parted teeth, enjoying every minute of it, wetting her lips with the tip of her tongue.

"I am," he boasted, "I'm the number one Lion... with two Super Bowl rings to prove it." Bo's lips stretched into a cocky smile.

Despite her growing desire, Lani had to strain to keep from laughing at his reference to being quarterback of the San Diego football team. She grabbed as much of his short hair as she could in her fist and squeezed firmly

# Conquering Embrace

but not hard enough to hurt him. Drawing his face close she murmured, "And does the king of beasts intend to make his own kill, or let the lioness do all the work?"

Bo's hazel eyes sparkled, his smile softened, and his chest swelled against her. Lani felt her senses ignite.

"The hunt is over, darling. I've tracked you down and now it's time to savor my prey," he breathed huskily as his lips descended to her slender throat. He nipped lightly at her flesh and Lani shivered, arching reflexively against him. She opened herself to him as if there were no tomorrow. Her passionate cries of fulfillment fueling his response.

His hands stroked and caressed. He pulled her tightly against his moist flesh. His mouth breathed hot against hers coaxing her onward. Lani swirled deeper and deeper into the throes of her desire and his words spiraled with her, trailing off, "Yes, darling, yes, you're all there is for me, all I'll ever want..."

# 6

THE SLANTING ORANGE rays of the morning sun streamed through the windows of Bo's bedroom, lighting on Lani's closed eyelids, softly rousing her from her deep sleep. Yawning, Lani stretched an arm across the large bed, reaching for Bo, only to find his half of the bed empty. Sitting up, she rubbed the sleep from her eyes and gazed about, hearing a gentle *whooshing* sound and seeing steam coming from the adjacent room.

Lani padded barefoot to investigate but the cool morning air against her naked flesh made her pause before Bo's open closet. Selecting one of his long-sleeved shirts, she quickly put it on. It hung almost to her knees providing just enough of a barrier against the morning chill.

She stepped into the next room to find a large, elegantly appointed bathroom: black tiled floor, blond wood paneling, a circular, Plexiglass-enclosed shower, and elaborate exercise equipment. Through large, partially opened glass doors, Lani saw a jacuzzi hot tub set in simple redwood decking. Bo was in the tub, sitting in the frothy, steamy water with his eyes closed, lost in private thought.

Venturing nearer, she started to announce her presence but something about Bo's meditative countenance made her pause. As he languished in the hot water, Lani saw him begin a series of stretching motions, moving slowly, painfully. He sat up and gripped one fist in the other, pulling hard with his arms, twisting his torso, flexing his muscles. The water glistened off his lean, taut torso. With each stretching motion, his face grimaced. He breathed heavily, grunting occasionally. As he twisted again, the morning light caught and highlighted a clean but long scar across one shoulder. She hadn't noticed it before. Her mind flashed back to the ugly bruise she had seen on Bo's knee when she visited him in the team locker room yesterday.

Seeing Bo go through these contortions, Lani wondered how long his magnificent body could take the kind of punishing abuse he put himself through every week of the football season. She continued to stare at his magnificent body with a combination of awe and bewilderment. The strain on his face, the long scar, his shining wet torso, the image of his badly bruised knee, effected her like a strong elixir, fascinating her, making her heart beat fast and hard.

She saw him open his eyes and, spotting her, break into a broad grin. "Hi, sleepyhead, I didn't want to wake you so I thought I'd start by myself, nothing like a hot bath to get things loosened up in the morning," he said, leaning back in the bubbly water. "C'mon in, Lani, the water's fine but I'm finer," he coaxed with a sly wink.

She moved toward the tub but, after taking a step up the platform, she stopped. "Bo, I couldn't help noticing your stretching exercise, are you all right, I mean are you in a lot of pain?" she asked, trying to sound matter of fact but there was no hiding the concern in her voice.

Bo's smile faded momentarily. "Not at all, Lani. It

# Conquering Embrace 81

just takes a little while to get all the kinks out in the morning. Don't worry about it, I'm fine, really. C'mon, get in."

Lani remained unconvinced, sure that Bo was hurting. "Bo, how can you keep it up, playing when you obviously aren't well?" she demanded.

His brow furrowed and then his hand snaked out and grabbed her by the wrist. "C'mere," he ordered and playfully pulled her down into the water with a splash.

Lani shrieked as Bo grabbed her and put his arms around her. She squirmed away and stood up. The shirt, soaking wet, clung to her like a second skin. It was nearly transparent and showed her body's every detail. A murmur of appreciation escaped Bo's lips before he reached up and pulled her back down.

"You ready for a little breakfast?" he asked while cupping her breasts beneath the water.

"Mmmm," she sighed as the swirling, bubbling water churned around them. She looked into Bo's contented eyes and offered, "Let me fix it, just tell me what you want."

"No need," he answered, reaching behind him to the deck behind the tub. "I've already taken care of everything." He pulled up a bottle of chilled champagne, popped out the cork, and allowed the bubbly wine to fountain up from the bottle over their faces, while he laughed wickedly. After taking a long drink from the bottle, he reached behind him again and produced two champagne flutes. Bo poured out a measure for each of them. They clinked glasses and Lani took a sip of the sparkling wine. Then Bo stood up and, as the bath water dripped off his shining, naked flanks, he walked over to the corner of the patio where he retrieved a tray holding several plates covered with metal domes. Holding the tray on the palm of one hand, Bo held it in front of Lani and pulled off the covers with his other. *"Voilà,"* he said grandly.

Lani gazed at scrambled eggs, toast, juice, fresh strawberries and, of all things, raw oysters on the half shell. "Marvelous, Bo," she complimented as he placed the tray on the edge of the deck next to the tub. She wrapped the hand holding her glass around his neck and took a sip of champagne before placing a warm kiss on the corner of his mouth. "I'd better dress properly for this wonderful breakfast," she teased as she discarded the shirt and tossed it in a wet heap on the floor.

Bo laughed his approval before squeezing a wedge of lemon over an oyster and slurping it into his mouth. Lani followed suit, savoring the oyster, closing her eyes, and thoroughly enjoying the exquisite, tender delicacy.

An hour rushed past as fast as the tingling bubbles of the jacuzzi flooded across Lani's body. Before she knew it, it was time for her to get dressed for work and for Bo to get ready for practice.

Pulling on her clothes, Lani watched Bo, sitting on the edge of the bed, slowly, gingerly lifting his legs to tie on his shoes. It was obvious his knee still bothered him and even the hot soothing water of the jacuzzi hadn't fully alleviated the pain. He maintained a straight face but a nagging fear began to build in the pit of Lani's stomach, a fear that unless Bo got out of football soon, his body would succumb to the punishing demands of the game and he'd suffer irreparable injuries. Was he mature enough to quit before he lost his pride and dignity? Even though their frolic in the tub and the memory of last night's lovemaking spun Lani in a web of affection for Bo, this thread of doubt continued to linger deep within her.

They finished dressing and headed into the living room where the midmorning sun streamed through the windows, bathing everything in warm, bright light. King was stretched out on the floor, thoroughly enjoying a warmly lit patch. They started out the door when the phone rang and Bo went to answer it.

Standing in the front doorway with the gentle ocean breeze blowing through her hair, Lani tried to purge the nagging doubts that ate at her. She concentrated instead on Bo's unflagging confidence, his easy, fluid charm, the deft manner in which he carried himself. Surely he had that undefined quality that would allow him to make the right decisions at the right time. She had no reservations about Bo being anything but a professional. He may be a diamond in the rough, she thought, but he was definitely worth polishing into a media personality. But how would she handle her personal feelings. Once she started working with him would her desire and emotional attachment get in the way? One thing Lani knew for sure: She wanted him more than anything else. The way he made love to her made Lani feel alive and desired. And the way he held her in his arms made her feel protected and loved.

An idea flashed before her. What better way to start polishing him than to have him over for dinner. Over a casual meal she could discuss the ins and outs of the business without it seeming like a lecture session. She still remembered some of her family's recipes for exotic Polynesian dishes. Yes, she would thoroughly enjoy cooking some of her favorite food for this man.

A cold wetness against the back of her hand startled Lani and she knew King had just said good morning. She turned and saw the golden retriever sitting on his haunches, wagging his tail across the floor. "King, you naughty brute. Don't you know you shouldn't sneak up on people?" she laughed, patting the rambunctious canine on the head.

Bo walked up to them and clipped a leash to the dog's collar. "Too bad this morning has to end," Bo said as he put an arm around Lani's shoulders and kissed her lightly on the lips.

"Bo, how about letting me repay your hospitality," Lani began. "I'd like to make dinner for you. I've got recipes for some great Polynesian dishes that I know you'll love?"

"That sounds wonderful, Lani," Bo agreed as they reached her car.

"Good! How about tonight, say about seven, at my place?"

"Any other night but tonight, Lani. That call I just got was to remind me I've got to speak at a banquet tonight. Sorry," he offered apologetically as he held open the car door for her.

Lani's smile faded.

"It's the local Rotary Club," he explained. "They give these banquets every now and then. They support some great humanitarian causes, but these affairs usually involve a lot of back-slapping, jokes, and guys trying to score some tickets from me."

Lani couldn't hide her disappointment. "All right, some other time, I guess." But, as she started to get in the car, a germ of an idea formed. "Say, maybe this is an opportunity for me to get acquainted with the type of people who'll form your support after you retire. Would it be okay if I tagged along and watched you in the thick of your following?"

Bo smiled but shook his head. "I'd love to bring you tonight, Lani but I doubt you'll enjoy yourself. Believe me, I'd much rather spend the time with you, but duty calls. If it's not too late, I'll call you afterwards."

"Sure, Bo, whatever," Lani replied, slumping into the driver's seat.

Bo closed the door and leaned his elbows against the car. "I had a wonderful time, Lani. I don't intend for it to be the last time, either," he assured her as he stroked the slender column of her throat before leaning down and giving her a soft, parting kiss on her lips.

Lani looked up into his warm hazel eyes, flashing a smile. "I guess I'll just have to curl up with a good book," she relented, firing up the Mustang's engine. She waved good-bye and pulled out of the driveway.

"Don't get too involved with it, I may get off early," he yelled after her.

\* \* \*

# Conquering Embrace

Lani arrived at her office, after stopping at her home to change her clothes. She shrugged off her shoulder bag, buzzed Joyce for a cup of coffee and half-heartedly began to wade into the pile of chores waiting for her.

This morning was particularly quiet and Lani breathed easy as the hours passed and no one called to demand her attention. It was rare that things went so smoothly. In place of the usual confusion that prevailed, Lani found herself remembering her wonderful evening with Bo. The passion that had charged her senses had faded into a soothing tranquility and she felt calmer than she had in weeks. Even several cups of overcooked coffee didn't put an edge on her peaceful composure.

She found herself looking far into the future, toying with images of she and Bo, intertwined in a life of happiness and passion. She could still taste the salty brine of his lips when they kissed on the cliffs with the surf crashing around them. The warmth of his enveloping arms, the beat of his heart against her bosom, were still vivid memories.

Running a pencil line through some particularly awful dialogue in a script for a popular brand of panty hose, Lani's mind drifted off the page and back to Bo's house. She closed the script, and penned a note, with a few biting suggestions for a rewrite, to the cover before tossing it onto a pile of other rejects.

Lani swiveled around in her chair, spotted the morning paper on her coffee table, and reached for it. As she thumbed through the paper, her thoughts continued to linger on Bo. Why had she fallen for this athlete, this super jock? There was no denying the powerful allure of his beautiful physique. A small smile stretched across her lips as she recalled the feel of his rippling torso under her fingers. But there was more to her feelings for Bo than just this physical attraction. There was something about the way his soothing words combined with his probing emerald and brown eyes. He had an inner strength that drew Lani over the brink of physical infatuation, to that deeper, undefined region reserved for love.

Lani idly flipped through the paper until she stopped at the sports page. Typically, it featured an article on the Lion's upcoming game, and mentioned their "old man" quarterback. Skimming through the article, Lani learned that Bo was fully recovered from last year's shoulder surgery. But there was still some concern for his battered knee. Evidently Lani wasn't alone in her feelings of anxiety over Bo's injuries. She remembered the time she'd badly twisted an ankle in a college tennis tournament. It hurt like hell and the resultant swelling nearly caused her to faint. But it was an important match, the conference championship, and if Lani's team was to win, she had to play. The trainer taped the ankle tightly and Lani gritted her teeth and played out her match. But even today, years later, the memory of the stabbing pain burned fresh in her mind each time she pivoted for a stroke. She was hobbled on crutches for two weeks afterwards and here was Bo, getting pounded every week, shrugging off the pain in pursuit of playing and winning, year after year. Sure, that was the mark of a professional athlete, she realized, but could she stand to see him go through those games knowing how badly he could be hurt? She absently rubbed her ankle as she finished the article.

Folding the sports page, she tossed it away. Then she buzzed her secretary. "Joyce, what's good to read?"

Joyce's voice answered through the desktop speaker, "You mean like fiction?"

"Right, something that doesn't require too much thinking, just something to keep my mind occupied in bed," Lani suggested.

"How about something that includes dinner and a bunch of loud, dumb jokes," a masculine voice suddenly broke in over the speaker.

"What? Charlie, what gives?" Lani asked after realizing that her boss was outside her office, at Joyce's desk.

The door to Lani's office clicked open and Charlie

## Conquering Embrace 87

strode through, trailing a cloud of thick, pungent cigar smoke. "The Rotary Club meeting tonight," he continued, sitting on her couch and putting his feet up on the coffee table.

Lani pinched her nose at the smell of the cigar.

"Joyce!" she yelled through the still open door. "I hate those things Charlie, it's bad enough our director, George smokes them on the set, now you're here stinking up my office," Lani complained but, as she expected, he merely kept the long cigar between his lips and began to thumb through the discarded newspaper.

Joyce entered and Lani, still holding her nose, pointed at Charlie and his fuming cigar. With a knowing smile, Joyce reached out and plucked it from his lips and carried the cigar out of the office, repeating what was obviously a regular ritual.

Charlie raised his eyebrows in mock surprise before easing back on the couch and putting down the paper. "I assume you and Cornell are working things out all right?"

"I guess you could say that," Lani replied. "He seems very interested in discussing ideas for marketing his name and reputation," she answered, choosing to keep the discussion on a purely business level.

"Good, good," Charlie answered. "You know about the Rotary Club meeting then?"

"He mentioned it," Lani answered, wondering what he was getting at. "Why?"

"I just thought that since I'm attending, maybe you'd like to come along, get to see our hero in action. It should be a good opportunity to see how the fans react in their own watering hole, so to speak."

"I'd heard," she replied, recalling Bo's description of the affair, "that it was going to be pretty boring."

He sat up and walked over to her, "I'll pick you up at seven-thirty. In this business, there's a lot of business *and* a lot of pleasure. But it's *always* business before pleasure and tonight I hope to have the pleasure of having you with me while we do a little business." Then he softened his hard line and gave her a little, begrudging smile. "Okay, Lani, please?"

"Oh, sure, okay," she answered, shaking her head, smiling at his tact.

"Great. I knew you'd understand," he replied before heading out the door. "Joyce, my cigar if you please," he called out as he closed the door behind him.

Lani reached for the half empty coffee cup on her desk. It looked like she'd be attending the Rotary Club function after all, and that meant being with Bo sooner, she realized, smiling to herself.

# 7

EVEN FROM THE parking lot, Lani could hear the noise generated by the assembly of Rotarians, shouting greetings, exchanging belly laughs. Peering out of the window of Charles' stylish but sensible sedan, Lani saw a simple hall and a surrounding parking lot. Several people, couples and single men, meandered about, slowing filtering into the building. Pulling down the passenger side sun visor and peering into the little mirror hung on the back, Lani stroked on a light coating of clear lip gloss. She licked her lips slightly, giving them a seductive sheen. The clear gloss allowed the light brown hue of her lips to show through and Lani liked the way her skin tone contrasted with her aquamarine-colored, chiffon dress. The billowy fabric was probably a little lightweight for the evening air but Lani liked the way the color worked with her eyes and the fabric hinted at her curves. Her only jewelry was a choker of tiny white pearls adorning her slender throat. She was carrying her natural off-white Mexican wool wrap.

Charlie opened her door and Lani was greeted by the brisk night air. She placed the wrap around her shoulders and turned to see Charlie staring at her.

He broke into a smile. "I must say, Lani, I've got the most lovely date here." He punctuated the praise with a wink.

He started to take her arm and Lani realized her open-toe sling-back high heels put her at near eye level with him. She liked the feeling of height, to say nothing of the way the shoes arched her ankles, accentuating her well-defined calves. Lani knew she looked good tonight and she felt bolder because of it. "Business before pleasure, Charlie, remember?" she teased, with a wink of her own.

"All I did was offer a simple but sincere compliment. Don't let it go to your head," he countered, holding out his arm.

Lani slipped her arm through and they joined the flow into the hall.

Inside, the high-ceilinged room was filled with people milling about, ordering drinks, exchanging war stories. As she expected, Lani saw clouds of blue cigar smoke rising upward. The walls featured various plaques and certificates proclaiming the many public-minded projects the Rotarians were involved in. A few odds and ends, such as a rack of deer antlers, a moose head, and some rather large, stuffed game fish, decorated the rafters, giving the hall a decidedly masculine air.

Across the room, Lani saw a raised dais, with a speaker's podium and tables situated on either side. Several people stood near this central fixture and Lani caught sight of a figure with short dark brown hair and rugged features. She continued to stare and realized it was Bo. He was chatting casually with the half dozen people gathered around him.

# Conquering Embrace 91

"There's our boy," Charlie said spotting Bo. "How about introducing me?"

Before she could answer, Charlie steered her in Bo's direction. As they approached, Lani noted Bo's stately bearing. He exuded an almost photo-perfect charm. His navy blue blazer and light gray slacks hung well from his trim, athletic frame. The way his torso funneled into a trim waist and tapered down his muscular, lean thighs made Lani's pulse quicken. Goosebumps prickled at the back of her neck.

Lani's attention suddenly shifted to a vivacious blond approaching Bo. The woman beamed a broad smile and planted an abundant greeting kiss on his cheek, close to his mouth.

He returned what appeared to be an equally warm greeting and Lani's grip on Charlie's arm tightened reflexively.

Bo spotted Lani and straightened his casual posture before smiling in her direction. His hesitation was only momentary, but Lani caught the subtle change in his demeanor. She felt a slight tremor in her bosom as she and Charlie reached Bo.

"Lani, this is a surprise... You look fantastic," Bo announced and leaned over to kiss her hello. Lani turned slightly and his lips grazed her cheek. She felt Charlie squeeze her arm, reminding her he was standing there.

"Oh, uh, Bo, I'd like you to meet Charlie, Charles Wordly. He's one of the founding fathers of our agency and also my boss," Lani offered, trying not to stare at the blond.

"Nice to meet you," Bo said as he shook Charlie's hand.

Bo, in turn introduced the blond. "Lani, Charles, I'd like you to meet Sheryl Canning, a good friend and a top-notch artists' representative, or so she tells me," he joked. The woman offered Lani her hand and Lani shook it indifferently, flashing a bewildered look at Bo. But he seemed to be looking in every direction but her's.

Charlie turned to Bo. "So, Lani tells me you're considering retiring from football after this season?" he asked, breaking the tension Lani felt building.

"Uh, perhaps. I haven't really decided yet," Bo answered as if he was in a fog.

Lani shifted her gaze from him and noticed Sheryl giving her the once over.

"Judging from what I've seen of the rushes of the sherry commercial," Charlie stated, "you might do quite well as an actor. With the right handling, you could fashion a very lucrative career."

"Lani, I like the way your boss thinks." Bo laughed, folding his arms across his chest.

Lani merely nodded in acknowledgment, uncomfortable in the presence of the Canning woman. "Ladies and gentlemen." Lani turned to the speaker's dais and saw a rotund, white-haired man, leaning into the microphone, "If you'll take your seats, dinner will be served and the proceedings will begin."

Bo seemed to breath a sigh of relief as he turned to her. "Guess we'll have to continue this later. Duty calls." With a nod of his head, he turned and strode to a table at the side of the speaker's platform.

"I think our table's this way, Lani," Charlie said as he took her arm and guided her to a seat. No sooner had she sat down before a little card marked, *Wordly,* then Lani saw the Canning woman seated directly across from her.

A battery of waitresses served up a simple but tasty dinner. A constant chatter continued as various Rotarians took their turn at the microphone. The mood of the affair was light and informal and occasionally the gathering would erupt in raucous laughter. Everyone seemed to be having a good time. But, despite the festive nature, Lani couldn't relax. Every time she looked at Sheryl Canning, her stomach seemed to contract.

Bo was called up as the featured speaker and, as he

took his place before the microphone, Lani watched Sheryl applaud. The woman literally gushed with enthusiasm.

A waitress set a cup of chocolate mousse before Lani while Bo began his speech, thanking the Rotarians for inviting him to speak. He cited some of their noteworthy public service works and then shifted into a discussion of football and its similarity to various aspects of life: The only way to score was to fight for every inch. Like a well-drilled football team, he continued, the Rotarians were a group of dedicated individuals with the pride and desire to do just that. The crowd loved it and it seemed that every line Bo delivered was met by applause. He peppered his speech with some fairly tame jokes, all met by exuberant laughter.

Lani marveled at Bo's total command of the group and how he stood before them, effortlessly exuding the same wit and charm that she witnessed during the sherry commercial. It seemed that whatever the situation, be it a tiring film shoot or speaking before a gathering of raucous Rotarians, Bo handled it with ease.

Toward the end of his speech, Bo announced the award for the ten boys and girls from various San Diego schools who excelled in sports while maintaining high grades and performing notable deeds, such as raising money with paper drives, selling candy bars to help their schools finance special education programs or buy athletic uniforms. Lani couldn't help but admire Bo as he stood there reading out the kids' achievements, shaking their hands and handing each of them a check for a hundred dollars.

At the conclusion of Bo's speech, Lani saw Sheryl Canning turn toward a couple seated next to her and loudly proclaim how it was her idea to include the kids' award presentation into the proceedings. The woman's tone was full of self-congratulatory back-patting as she continued saying she picked the particular photographer to snap the photos of Bo presenting the checks. Nothing but the best for her client, she said finally. The mousse suddenly turned to chalk on Lani's tongue and she tossed her spoon into the serving dish with a loud clang.

The more Lani witnessed Sheryl Canning's efforts to indicate her tight link with Bo, the more the nervous knot in Lani's stomach tightened. As soon as the waitresses took away the last of the desserts, the multitude of smokers lit up and swirls of stifling blue smoke wafted upward. The loud discussions and laughter continued and the room got stuffier and stuffier.

Charlie put his napkin back on the table and turned toward Lani. "I've got to ask the officers a few questions, Lani, but I'll be right back." Sliding back his chair, he walked up to the speaker's platform.

A cup of coffee appeared before her and Lani welcomed the hot dark brew, sipping it gingerly to remove the taste of the mousse.

Lani shifted her gaze around the room and saw Bo chatting with the teenagers who received the awards.

"Miss Richards."

Lani turned to see Sheryl Canning leaning her elbows on the table, facing her.

"Yes?" Lani answered, setting down her cup.

"I understand from Bo that you two have worked together recently," the woman said flatly.

"That's right," Lani affirmed. "I supervised a commercial Bo did for my company."

The woman knit her brow while studying Lani with an unsettling scrutiny. "Perhaps he mentioned me to you. I'm an artists' representative, an agent if you will."

"No, I'm afraid not." Lani answered evenly, shifting her gaze to the nearby waitress, signaling her cup was ready for a refill.

"Well," the woman continued, "it seems we both have a professional interest in Mr. Cornell. You see, Bo and I have discussed his breaking into the media and I must say, he seemed very receptive to my ideas. It's not often I come across such a natural. I'm sure he'll do well."

Lani wasn't sure where this woman was heading with this discussion, but she didn't care for her smug, tone.

"Yes, I think he'll do just fine," Lani agreed, just as smugly.

"Well," Sheryl continued, her brown eyes beginning to glint, as if she were enjoying stringing her point out slowly, "the reason I bring this up is I'm going to be representing Bo in his business affairs."

Lani felt the knot in her stomach twist and stretch. She noted the look of satisfaction that appeared on the woman's face. If this were true, why hadn't Bo mentioned it to her? Lani hadn't expected he would keep such a secret, not after the intimacies they had shared recently.

"You see, it's possible you and I may be working together, on different sides of the fence, of course," Sheryl said. "I just wanted you to know that if there's anything I can do for you regarding Bo's future plans, you can feel free to give me a call and we can set up a meeting." The woman's voice was sickeningly sweet.

Lani set her coffee cup down harder than she realized. The porcelain china cup hit the saucer sharply and liquid spilled out and over the tablecloth. Lani inwardly chided herself for reacting to this woman's boasting, but this news caught her off guard and she could do little more than stare back, incredulously, waiting for the woman to continue.

Sheryl then pulled a small wallet from her purse and fished out a card. Extending it toward Lani she continued, "Here's my card, Miss Richards. I'll be handling *all* of Bo's business affairs, so I can handle all of your questions."

Lani found herself taking the business card dumbly. The loud din of the Rotarians, combined with the waves of acrid smoke, made Lani's head ache, her eyes water, and her throat dry. The temperature in the room seemed to rise several degrees. With the arrogant blond in such close proximity, Lani wanted more than anything else to grab a few breaths of fresh air.

Picking up her woolen wrap, she turned toward Sheryl Canning and, still holding the card, stood up. "I'll remember your offer, Miss Canning. If you'll excuse me." Without waiting for a reply, Lani walked purposefully away from the table.

Outside the hall Lani slowed her pace and welcomed the chill evening air. She crossed over the clipped soft lawn, continued across the peaceful park, and took in several deep breaths, trying to regain her composure. The gall of the woman, Lani reflected in anger. Lani had encountered her pushy type before in her business dealings but the woman's presence was so unexpected, and the fact that she and Bo were cohorts, ate at Lani's insides like acid.

Strolling toward a low stone bench, Lani sat down and directed her gaze to the city lights in the distance. Overhead the sky was clear and several stars twinkled vigilantly.

She focused her gaze on the lights trying to rid her mind of the swirl of puzzling, unsettling thoughts. But the questions continued to plague her, demanding answers. Lani realized she still held Sheryl's card in her hand, and she crumpled it up and tossed it toward a clump of nearby bushes. Why hadn't Bo mentioned that he had already chosen an agent? What was he trying to prove? Lani remembered their dinner and Bo entertaining the waitress' advances. Was that it, was Lani just another groupie to him? Could he possibly be playing Lani against Sheryl? Was that how his ego worked? Did he simply want to add her to his stable of adoring female fans? Surely he didn't think her interest in him was that shallow.

"Lani... there you are."

The voice broke her train of thought and Lani turned toward it with a start. She saw Bo, striding lazily up to her, grinning broadly.

"For a minute there, I'd thought you'd left." He placed a gentle hand on the back of her neck and leaned down to kiss her.

Lani remained motionless. It was obvious from the

way that Bo pulled away that he sensed that something was wrong.

"Lani, is anything wrong?" he asked in his unsettling, calm manner. Not answering, she shifted her attention back to the distant lights.

Undaunted, Bo continued, "I did warn you after all that these affairs were boring."

How could he be so ignorant of her feelings, Lani wondered. Unable to keep her unanswered questions inside any longer, Lani turned to face him. "Bo, why didn't you tell me you had an agent?"

"My agent? You mean Sheryl?" he asked feigning innocence.

"Well, who else do you think I mean? She even went so far as to suggest I have a meeting with her if I had any questions about your affairs."

Bo emitted a short laugh and then sat down on the bench beside Lani. "I guess Sheryl is a bit pushy about her job," he said taking Lani's hands between his. "Your hands are so cold, Lani..." He rubbed them lightly and continued, "Sheryl's not my agent. I would've told you if that were true. That's just her style, you know, trying to beat out the competition."

"I wasn't aware there was competition for your services," Lani replied coldly.

Bo's smile faded. "I've got to keep my options open, Lani. I thought you'd be the first to understand that I've got to direct my career in the best way possible. There's nothing wrong with talking with Sheryl and seeing what she can suggest regarding the handling of my affairs after I quit playing football."

Lani withdrew her hands from between his. "So what did you intend to do, hear what I had to offer and then weigh it against her suggestions while you got a little 'action' on the side?"

"Lani, I think you're overreacting. It's not like that at all." His tone was even but his eyes bored deeply into her.

Lani didn't want to sit there and argue with Bo, so she stood up. "I don't know how it is, Bo, all I know is that there's something funny going on and I'm not sure what to believe anymore." She turned and walked a few steps across the soft grass trying to hide her rising emotional turmoil.

"Lani..." he called after her.

"Just drop it, Bo, okay," she called back over her shoulder, taking a few more steps away from him. The lights in the distance began to blur as tears started to well up in Lani's eyes. How could Bo consider a pushy, self-centered agent, in the same league as herself? Lani folded her arms across her chest, hugging herself tightly, trying to stave off the anger that continued to build up inside her. Had she been such a fool? She had allowed herself to become more and more involved with Bo, forgetting about business and now here he was, putting business between them. How could he play such a terrible game with her?

Suddenly she felt his presence behind her, his breath hot against her neck. "You're not giving me much of a chance to explain, Lani. Don't you think I deserve a little more than that?"

Lani turned to face him. Even in the soft light from the few scattered lamps in the park, she could see Bo's emerald-brown stare questioning her. He placed his hands on her shoulders and gently tried to draw her toward him. Lani's gaze shifted to his full, curving lips, his squared chin, his sculpted features. The furrow between his eyebrows relaxed and Lani felt herself slowly being drawn inward by his magnetism. As if sensing her submission, Bo's eyes glinted knavishly and his lips seemed to stretch into what she thought was a triumphant grin. "You're really quite beautiful, Lani, much too attractive to spoil with silly frowns. There's no need to be jealous, honey."

The words somehow hit a nerve and all Lani could think about was his smug attitude in thinking she was

## Conquering Embrace

merely jealous, and could be placated by a few soothing words from a dashing Galahad, with a crew cut and a quick smile. Did he really believe she could be swayed so easily, as if nothing at all had happened to upset her? Bo's features became hazy as Lani's anger rose. She would not be an easy mark for this man, who felt as comfortable in a lady's bedroom, as he did in shoulder pads.

Lani put the heels of her hands against his chest and pushed trying to escape his grasp. "Try your smooth lines somewhere else, Bo. I'm not buying any of it!"

A nearby commotion made them both hesitate and turn their heads to see a couple approaching. The man seemed to be fumbling for his keys while his stiffly coiffed wife chastised him about always losing everything and she'd never let him forget it if they kept the baby-sitter waiting again. The couple eventually passed them, and Lani used the interruption to break Bo's grip. She marched toward the hall. The stuffy room full of loud Rotarians suddenly seemed preferable to standing outside arguing with Bo.

"Lani, you're being childish. Wait a minute," Bo called after her, but she kept walking toward the hall. She heard his footsteps, padding quickly across the grass and suddenly she felt his hand grasp her wrist. Lani tugged away from him, but rather than let go, Bo pulled harder, encircling her waist with his arms, and holding her fast against his muscled torso. "Stop it, Lani! Look at me," he demanded and she slowly tilted her head to meet his fierce smoldering gaze. The confident smile had disappeared from his lips.

"Let's quit this playacting, shall we?" he commanded, his breath searing her cheek. Desire seemed to exude from his every pore and Lani's headstrong determination to pull away began to melt.

"From that first day on the set, I knew I had to have you, Lani, not just to put you in my stable, as you might put it, but to love and have you with me, aside from everything else. I don't want anyone else. I want you, Lani."

"I... I want to believe you," Lani heard herself say.

"You can, Lani. I've never been more sure of anything in my whole life," he replied, taking the soft point of her chin between his thumb and forefinger and gently tilting her mouth up to meet his. His fiery stare softened and Lani murmured a soft sigh of pleasure as she threw her arms around his neck, responding to her rising heartbeat and the ache she felt for him. She met his soft full lips with her own and was caught up in the bliss, recalling their passionate moments the night before.

His tongue probed gently against her lips and Lani parted them. A low moan of pleasure rose from her throat and she pressed close against him, feeling his heart beat in rhythm with her own.

Out of breath, they slowly drew apart, and Bo buried his face in the soft curls behind her ear, gently nipping the lobe with his teeth. Lani responded, kissing the side of his throat, running her fingers over the short, bushy hair at the back of his head. "Oh, Bo," she murmured, "why is it always so hard for two people to wade through all their differences before realizing how much they really want each other?" she said, not expecting an answer but merely reflecting on the way lovers always seem to experience such difficulties.

"It's just the way people are, I guess, Lani. Nobody ever said love was supposed to be easy," he replied, breathing a contented sigh. "I'm sorry things didn't work out so well tonight, but after all, I did warn you," he teased.

"Yes, you did, Bo, but then I didn't realize you meant something besides the Rotary banquet." Lani couldn't help blurting out the reference to Sheryl Canning. Bo responded with a frown.

"Yes, well, that isn't what I meant, but now that it's out in the open, I expect we can deal with it like intelligent adults." His tone was that of a teacher to a pupil and the memory of their fiery kiss was suddenly replaced by Lani's resentment at being treated like a little girl. Bo seemed to sense her irritation because he quickly changed his tactics.

"Look, the team has some free time this weekend and I've got a cabin in the mountains. How about you and I driving up with King and go spend a nice quiet little vacation together?"

It was a tempting proposition but her mixed feelings for Bo's covert dealings with Sheryl made Lani hesitate. The last few days with him had been intense and now, with her emotions raw and vulnerable, Lani wondered if maybe too much time together would foster more tension. She couldn't deny her feelings for him, but how often would she find herself becoming lost in passionate bliss, only to be sobered by his smug tone, to become irritated and alienated from him?

"Bo, it sounds like a wonderful idea but... well, maybe we're spending too much time together. You know what I mean? Maybe we need a little time apart, to think things out, get a little room to breathe," Lani suggested reluctantly.

"You might be right, darling, but this is the only weekend I'll have free until the season's over. Besides, I'm not sure I can stand to be without you for a whole weekend," he cajoled, his lips forming a silly grin.

Still uncertain, Lani hesitated.

"C'mon, Lani, there's a beautiful lake, lots of streams, nobody around for miles... it'll be great. And if we run out of things to do we can always discuss your ideas on marketing my name. What do you say?"

The thought of discussing business with Bo, knowing he would still court Sheryl's offer, struck a sensitive chord in Lani. "In that case, maybe we'd better invite Sheryl to come along and offer her expertise," she suggested bitterly.

"Oh, boy. I can see you've got a sensitive nerve exposed tonight. Let's just forget about her, okay?" Lani could hear the annoyance in his voice.

"Does that mean she's out as far as handling your business affairs?" Lani asked tauntingly.

Bo stood back and placed his hands on his hips, shaking his head. "I don't know what's the matter with you, Lani. Just because I keep a few avenues open for suggestions, you fly off the handle. I can't afford to ignore anything or anybody if there's a chance they can help me plan my future to the best advantage. Surely you can understand that."

Bo made it sound so simple. In many ways, he was right, but then again, he used his smooth pitch to get her involved with him in the first place.

"I can understand, Bo. I just don't like being deceived, that's all."

"Look, it would mean a lot to me if you'd come up to the mountains. Give me a chance to prove how much I care for you," he continued, softening his tone.

Lani stared deeply into Bo's eyes and saw his sincerity. But the thought that he could consider Sheryl Canning her professional equal gnawed at Lani's insides. She wanted nothing more than to spend the weekend with him, but she wouldn't be able to live with herself if she couldn't make Bo see through that woman's shallow, pushy facade. If she had to fight fire with fire, Lani would do it. Setting her lips with a sly smile of her own, she replied, "All right, Bo, I'll go, but don't expect miracles."

His face mirrored his relief. "Wonderful, darling, that's all I ask. We'll have a terrific time, you'll see." He started to lean forward to kiss her but approaching voices interrupted them again.

"Bo, there you are, I've been looking all over for you," Sheryl called as she traipsed toward them, followed by a couple of Rotarians, still holding drinks in their hands.

"Just getting a little fresh air and enjoying the company of my friend," Bo replied, turning toward them.

"Well, come on, old boy," one of the Rotarians said, placing an arm around Bo's shoulders, "we've still got one more award for you to hand out. Please excuse us, m'am," he said to Lani, while pulling Bo back toward the hall. Bo went off with them, shrugging his shoulders at Lani. Sheryl followed after them.

Lani could care less. She had already set her mind on what she had to do. As their voices faded in the distance, Lani contemplated just how she'd bring that cocky quarterback into line. She'd have *him* alone for the weekend and his education would begin. She'd make it tough and when she was done, Bo would understand just what a taskmaster she could be. Strolling back toward the hall, Lani smiled to herself. By the time she was done with Bo he'd understand the tough life a media personality faced and there'd be no doubt about which woman offered the best in terms of business expertise.

# 8

STARING OUT OF the passenger window, Lani watched the brush-covered, rolling hills outside San Diego gradually give way to pine-studded, green forests. Beside her, Bo diligently kept his silence, only occasionally making a comment about the view, the fun they'd have at the cabin, the chance to be alone together to unwind from the city grind. But Lani wasn't interested in small chitchat and after several indifferent replies to Bo's attempts to open up a conversation, he left her alone. Only King's wet nose, bussing her cheek as he leaned through the rear window of the cab from the campershell-enclosed truck bed, could bend Lani from her vigilant staring through the window.

It was true that she wanted to be alone with Bo, away from her work, the traffic and crowds, but her need to straighten him out on just where she stood with regard to her professional ability was a nagging priority, and she couldn't imagine being able to relax and enjoy the solitude of the woods until this was settled.

During the four hours they'd been driving, she glanced periodically at Bo as he maneuvered the able but battered truck over the rough, rural roads that led to the mountains. In his faded jeans, dusty boots, and frayed flannel shirt with its torn sleeves rolled up to his forearms, he appeared much as he did that first day on the set when his carefree and brassy demeanor struck Lani so negatively.

The road began to incline steeply and Bo grabbed the floor shift and moved it several times before he managed to engage the four-wheel drive. With an affectionate pat on the dashboard, he pushed down on the accelerator, the truck gave a lurch and rambled slowly up the steep mountain road.

Already the sun was beginning to dip low in the sky, sending streaks of light filtering through the branches of the ever thickening green forest. They continued to climb and Lani put her hands under her red and gray, woolen ski sweater, trying to warm them.

"We should be getting there pretty soon, Lani," Bo said, reaching over to switch on the heater. "It's getting dark pretty fast. I doubt I can find the place without sunlight. There aren't any streetlamps where we're going."

Lani turned with a start and looked hard at Bo. His silly smile indicated he was obviously joking. She turned back to the window, continuing to ignore him. Besides, she thought to herself, the wooded beauty outside held plenty to keep her mind occupied.

Overhead, the tops of the tall, majestic pines glinted green against the still blue sky, while on the ground, the truck groaned its way through the ever darkening shadows.

"We must be getting close," Bo judged as he leaned forward and squinted through the windshield. Following his gaze, Lani straightened up in her seat, anxious for

## Conquering Embrace 107

the long drive to be over so she could finally stretch her legs.

"There we go, looks like we made it," Bo said as Lani spotted a solitary A-frame cabin, nestled in a small clearing surrounded by towering fir trees. Bo pulled the truck up to the rustic, wood-sided cabin and shut off the engine.

"Finally," Lani breathed aloud as she opened the door and slid down to the pine needle-covered ground. She was instantly hit by the cold mountain air and her teeth began to chatter.

"It's not the Ritz, but I'd say right now, it's the next best thing," Bo remarked as he moved past her, carrying their groceries and opening the front door. Lani's only reply was to stomp her feet on the ground, trying to get some circulation going.

Bo came back out of the cabin and walked past Lani to the tailgate and pulled out their bags. Meanwhile, King leaped from the truck and raced over the needle-blanketed ground, sniffing from tree to tree, exploring the new territory.

Bo peered around and then pointed to something between the trees. "Look over there, Lani."

She gave a perfunctory glance but the incredible sight of a crystal blue lake, shining through the branches, took her breath away.

"It's beautiful," she admitted and saw Bo's face light up at her words.

Bo filled his lungs with air and exhaled loudly. "This mountain air is terrific, Lani, really clears out your head."

He was right. She could almost taste the fresh, clean air. It was certainly a welcome change from the awful city fumes she was used to.

It was a beautiful setting but even so Lani still felt uneasy about things. She wasn't ready to forget her reason for coming. "It's pretty cold, Bo. I'm going inside," she said, leaving him to follow her with the rest of their gear.

Stepping across the wood floor, Lani found the simple kitchen and emptied the bags of groceries Bo had brought in. In the dimming light she could see the room had a rustic charm. It featured several wooden cabinets, an ancient looking ice box and a small gas range. She moved to the main room and noted the high, loft ceiling, held up by rough-hewn beams and illuminated by the A-shaped windows that extended to the peak of the roof. It was a lot like Bo's home, although much more primitive. A loft bedroom completed what was basically one large room with a small bathroom tucked away in a corner. Lani brushed her hand over the wall looking for a light switch but found none.

"No electricity..." Bo called out as he lugged in the cooler from the truck and began to feed it's contents into the ice box.

"I don't suppose there's any gas, either?" Lani answered rubbing her arms against the chill.

"There's propane for cooking but mostly it's just us and the elements. But once I build a fire it'll be nice and cozy. Besides, who needs the amenities of civilization when we've got each other," he teased, leaning down for a kiss. Lani wasn't in a joking mood and turned away.

Bo stuck a match into the wick of a hurricane lantern. In the lamp's yellow light, he moved to the little hearth in the main room and proceeded to build a fire.

There was a small, hand ax stuck in a pile of logs at the side of the river rock hearth and as Bo bent to the task, he started whistling contentedly to himself.

His carefree manner, grated on Lani's nerves. She felt anything but at ease with so much left unresolved between them. Nevertheless, her eyes were drawn to him as he gripped the hatchet and swung it hard into the short logs, splitting them into kindling. The veined musculature of his well-defined hands stood out in the dim light and Lani found herself mesmerized by the rhythm of his strokes. He quickly had a mound of kindling and small faggots piled up in the hearth and put a match to the

## Conquering Embrace 109

creation. It flickered, caught, crackled, and licked up in flames.

"We'll have this place snug in no time," Bo assured her as he brushed splinters and soot from his hands and carried a load of wood upstairs, to build a fire in the small pot-bellied stove in the loft.

There was a scratch on the front door and Lani opened it to find King sitting on the door step, wagging his tail, ready to come in and get warm. Lani followed him to the fireplace and, with King curled up in front of it, she put her back to the warming hearth and rubbed her hands together behind her back.

Bo appeared with a bottle of brandy and two china cups. "A little something to warm up the insides?" he asked while pouring a stiff shot into each cup.

Lani took the offered cup. After a tentative sip she felt the amber liquid quickly burn a fiery path to her stomach. She winced slightly and looked up from her cup to see Bo staring at her expectantly.

"I'm glad you decided to come up here, Lani. We'll have a great time, believe me," he promised, taking a hefty slug from his cup.

"You've got it all worked out, have you?" Lani challenged.

Bo's eyes narrowed slightly. "Lani, what's the matter? Why are you so tense?" he asked, coming up and placing a hand on her shoulder. He put his cup on the hearth and with both hands, began to kneed the back of her neck. For a moment the pleasurable sensation, combined with the brandy and the warmth from the fire made Lani breath deeply and relax to the point where she nearly fell against him trying to steady herself. But the thought that it was too easy for Bo, that he must be thinking she was playing right into his hands, made her stiffen and move out of his grasp.

She took refuge on a small couch facing the hearth. Bo hesitated and she saw him look at her, bewildered, his jaw set as if he were starting to get annoyed. Good!

Lani thought to herself. If he thought she'd melt into his arms so easily, he had another think coming. After a moment, Bo walked over and sat beside her.

Leaning over, he whispered in her ear, "We've got the whole night to ourselves, Lani. There's no one around to knock on the door, no phone to ring, no coach to scream bloody murder, and your boss can't possibly get ahold of you."

He traced a path of soft kisses down the back of her neck with his lips. His breath was hot against her sensitive flesh, nearly making her swoon with the delicate sensation. What kind of maddening power did this man have that he could literally melt her determination with his passionate onslaught? she asked herself.

The soft flesh of his curving lips, his encircling arms holding her against him, and her own pounding heart were all working to sap her resolve. She knew that if she gazed into his intense, smoldering eyes she would be completely consumed.

Summoning the last of her inner determination, Lani slunk from his embrace and moved as far away as the little couch would allow.

"Don't you feel well, Lani? You're not car sick are you?" he asked, the annoyance in his voice building.

"No, I'm fine," she replied curtly, wondering just what it would take to shape him into line.

"Well..." he pondered, shaking his head and rising from the couch. "Maybe after a little dinner we'll both feel a little better."

From the couch, Lani heard him foraging around in the kitchen. She got up and found him lighting the stove. She pulled out some of their groceries, and they silently began preparing their meal, opening cans, getting out the pots and pans.

With conversation at a minimum, they prepared a simple but elegant little meal and Lani was surprised that she actually did feel a bit better afterwards. With a smug little smile to herself, Lani contemplated how she'd handle the smooth-talking quarterback.

## Conquering Embrace 111

Bo lit the propane-fired water heater and Lani did the dishes while he dried. Despite everything, Lani couldn't help being amused at the little domestic scene they'd created in the middle of this remote forest. She enjoyed playing house with Bo and, if she could straighten him out and deflate his arrogance, the concept could definitely have future potential.

The dishes finished, Lani grabbed a kerosene lantern, foraged around in her bag and dragged out a notebook and several paperbacks. Taking them with her to the couch, she sat down and began thumbing through the paperbacks, while enjoying the flickering warmth from the fireplace.

Bo was back with the china mugs, this time nearly full with steaming black coffee. "This ought to cap of the meal nicely," he mumbled while pulling the cork off the bottle of brandy and topping off each cup. The aromatic spirit, combined with the coffee, drifted across the little room, mixing with the distinctive smell of the burning wood, to give the cabin a coziness that Lani hadn't felt since she was a little girl living in Hawaii.

"What do you think of the place, Lani?" Bo asked idly, setting down his cup.

"I'll admit it's a lot better than I thought it would be," she said begrudgingly.

"I'm glad you like it. I built it myself," he proclaimed proudly.

"You're into just about everything," Lani commented rather flippantly, even though she was impressed.

"Not everything, Lani," he responded, catching her drift. "But some things, like building houses, or even just cabins, take skill, as well as time and a lot of hard work. It took three months just to lay up the stones for the fireplace. Believe me, carrying those rocks up from the river was harder than football practice. I almost quit several times, but it was worth it."

"I'm glad to see you're aware of the value of hard work, Bo. It'll be important when you decide to retire and make your living at something other than a kid's game," Lani responded cuttingly.

He got up and walked over to the hearth and stared into the flames. The orange light of the fire accentuated the rugged line of his jaw, silhouetting his trim, muscular frame. He finally turned back to her. "Lani, I'm not sure what's going on, but I feel that you're not at all comfortable here with me."

"I'm perfectly comfortable, Bo. It's just that there's a lot on my mind and I've got a lot of work to do."

"What are you talking about? This is supposed to be a chance for some R and R, you know, rest and relaxation?"

"First things first, then maybe there will be time for a little R and R," she countered, thumbing through the books, writing page numbers on her pad.

"Have you looked at the loft, yet?" he continued, "with the stove going, and us tucked under a couple of down sleeping bags, we'll be as snug as bugs." His tone was casual but there was no mistaking the wicked gleam that flashed from his eyes.

"Here, you might as well get started," she ordered ignoring his efforts to woo her upstairs, thrusting the paperbacks into his hands.

"What's this?" Bo replied, confused. He held the books up to catch the light from the fireplace. *"Contemporary Media Systems, Broadcasting: The Business and the Science, Reporting as a Career, On Acting and Actors,* seems like pretty dry stuff, Lani."

"I'm sure you'll find them quite involving once you start reading, Bo."

"You don't mean *now?*"

"Of course, why not? You've got to start somewhere and there's no better way to break into show business than to start at the beginning," she replied, fixing him with a determined stare.

"Why? Are you going to quiz me in the morning?" he countered with a note of sarcasm.

"That's not a bad idea," she answered. "I can't afford

to waste my time with someone who doesn't understand or care about the nuts and bolts of the game. Someone with your immeasurable talent shouldn't have any trouble grasping what's in those books."

"But I had a different idea of how we'd spend this weekend. I hadn't intended to come all the way up here just to pour over some books."

"It's up to you," Lani answered, undaunted, "but you'll never make it in show business if you don't learn the essentials. You can't be flippant about such details as showing up for a shoot on time, or appearing in public in the proper attire and especially about maintaining the proper decorum among so many fawning female fans."

"My style hasn't hurt me any so far," he answered defensively.

"Oh, you might get an occasional job plugging a product here and there, but it takes something extra to get the big jobs, representing top sponsors. You get the wrong reputation and the prestige companies will stay away from you like the plague. In case you didn't know it by now, I don't like to work with snobs or dunces," she added firmly.

"And what are you going to do while I sit here and read all night?"

"I feel awfully beat from that long drive. I think I'll turn in... alone. Besides, that'll give you plenty of time to read with no distractions." With a toss of her head she traipsed up the stairs to the loft.

"Lani, wait a minute," he called in exasperation.

"Good night, Bo," she called down, blowing out the lantern and getting undressed for bed.

"Well, if that don't beat all," she heard him mutter to the dog.

Lani pulled down the covers and started to get in the bed when she paused and went to the loft railing. Peering into the room below she saw Bo sitting before the fire, his dog at his feet, opening one of the books. The scene was vintage early America and Lani almost laughed out loud at the poster-like setting featuring her reluctant pupil.

She'd gauged his response accurately. Even though she ran the risk that her snubbing him might infuriate Bo, she took the chance, confident that he was still anxious to impress her. Faced with a simple ultimatum, he chose to go along with it rather than let her think he could care less about her ideas on business and professionalism.

The books were basic primers, providing the rudiments that were necessary for Bo to fully understand what he faced in the various areas of the media. Sure his looks and charm could carry him through a few jobs, but she'd seen other athletes try to break into such fields as sports broadcasting only to fail because they didn't understand exactly what they were doing. Reading this material could make a big difference between Bo being just another jock holding a microphone or climbing to the top. Besides, if he wasn't willing to work for his new image, she wasn't interested in him at all.

Satisfied, Lani jumped between the covers, pulled them tight around her neck and settled into a deep, comfortable sleep.

A series of muffled clanks and door closings broke through the fog of sleep and Lani opened her eyes and sat up, getting her bearings. Down below, Bo was clambering around in the kitchen. Rubbing the sleep from her eyes, Lani yawned loudly. "Bo, it's the middle of the night, what're you doing?" she yelled down.

"Rise and shine, sleepyhead," he answered in a jolly voice.

"You can't be serious," she groaned, leaning over to the bedside table and checking her wristwatch. It was barely five A.M.

"Time to get going, Lani. Those fish won't wait all day."

"Fishing?" she replied in disbelief. "It's still dark outside."

"Sun's coming up. By the time we reach the stream, it'll be bright and sunny. Let's get a move on, dear."

He seemed to take relish in rousing her so early, as if making up for last night. Any thoughts of ignoring him and going back to sleep were quickly dashed as King bounded onto the bed and gave her a cold good morning kiss with his tongue. Grabbing a robe and slippers, she went downstairs and found Bo pouring coffee and stuffing a medium-sized backpack.

He greeted her with a bemused smile, his eyes crinkling mischievously. "Ever been fly fishing?"

Lani took a long gulp of the surprisingly good coffee and shook her head negatively.

"You'll love it. Come on, throw on some clothes and let's go. We've got a couple of miles of hiking ahead of us."

Lani leaned against the kitchen counter and started to fall back asleep, but Bo was quickly beside her and she opened her eyes to see him gazing down on her, smiling and lightly appraising her sleepy contenance.

"You're truly beautiful in the morning, Lani," he whispered, grazing her lips with his own. But, before she could reply, he put his hands on her shoulders, stood her up, turned her around, and gently nudged her toward the stairs. "Hurry up, now, get dressed. Wear something comfortable that you can hike in."

Like a zombie, Lani climbed back upstairs to get dressed. Gulping down the last of the coffee, she wondered why she was putting up with this ordeal.

Falling in step behind Bo, Lani shivered in the cool mountain air. He strode purposefully ahead of her following a pine needle-covered path that meandered through the woods. Bo had the pack slung across his shoulders, while Lani carried two long skinny fishing poles. King went his own way, alternately following Bo and then darting off into the woods after rabbits and squirrels.

Lani was sure Bo was out to prove his macho fortitude in the wild and she was determined to keep him under a tight rein with plenty of lessons still in store for him.

Lani began to fall into her stride and her body quickly warmed with the exertion. The morning sun began to rise in the sky and, as Bo paused to scout out his direction, Lani stood in a patch of sunlight feeling it's warmth spread across her cheeks. She turned back to see Bo staring at her still wearing that silly smile.

"What's so funny?" Lani asked suspiciously.

"Oh, nothing in particular, just that scowl you're wearing, I guess."

"I'm not scowling."

"Whatever you say," he answered lazily, pulling off a branch from a small, berry covered shrub. "Lemon berry..." he said holding it out to her. Lani took it indifferently and examined the delicate little specimen. "Over there, that's wild cucumber and off to the side of it's buckwheat."

"My, you're quite the nature boy, right at home in the woods aren't you?" she answered haughtily, a bit annoyed with his nonchalance.

"You may not think too much of it, but I try to keep my eyes open. I appreciate the few things in this world that mean something," he reflected, unscrewing the top of a plastic canteen and taking a drink.

"I care about nature, Bo, I've spent many long afternoons with my grandfather enjoying the rain forests in Hawaii. It's just that right now, I'd think you'd be a little more concerned with making something out of your life after football." Her dig made him look hard at her.

"You read any of those books I gave you," she asked, as she took the canteen from him and drank from it.

"Sure, I read them. At least I skimmed through most of them. You going to quiz me now, teacher?" he asked sarcastically.

"Maybe. Think any of what was in those books will rub off on you?" she jabbed, tossing him the canteen.

## Conquering Embrace  117

"What's with this sudden attention to business, Lani? Can't you ease off a bit and enjoy the surroundings?"

"It's attention to business that makes me good at what I do, Bo, and it's time you started getting serious about it because you won't be playing football forever. Sooner or later you'll get tired of courting groupies or maybe they'll get tired of you when you're no longer a star," Lani fired back.

"There's a time and a place for everything, Lani. Don't worry, I'll be a good little student and follow teacher's orders...when it's appropriate. I'm not washed up yet," he snapped, clipping the canteen to his belt. "Right now we're in the middle of this wonderful forest, with no smog, no traffic noises, and no office buildings, so let's drop all this talk about business and get in some fishing while we've got the chance. C'mon, King, fish are waiting." He stalked away, up the trail.

Lani hadn't wanted to fight with him, but she'd made her point and, satisfied, she trailed after them.

After about twenty minutes, Bo stopped and cocked his head, listening intently. "Hear that, Lani?" he asked, extending a hand and pulling her up to him.

She listened and heard what sounded like a soft rush of wind, or crazily, a distant freeway.

Bo led her off the trail, through the overgrown forest. Using his arms to sweep aside thick branches, he led them to a bubbling stream, perhaps twenty feet across and so clear that in spots she could actually see shapes gliding through the rushing water. Leaves from an overhanging tree gently drifted down onto the water where they swirled around a half submerged rock.

"What do you think, Lani?" Bo whispered.

"It's beautiful," she replied. "Why are we whispering?"

"Don't want to scare the fish. Any little sound could spook them away," he said, unslinging his pack.

A rustle in the nearby brush on the other bank of the stream caught King's attention and the golden retriever stiffened and stared trying to get a fix on the sound. Bo darted out a hand and grabbed King's collar.

"Look's like he's caught the scent of some pheasant or maybe a quail. Next thing you know, he'll go tromping through the water and we probably won't see him again for the rest of the day," he explained, coaxing the anxious dog to sit down and relax.

Looking upstream, Lani saw how the water flowed over rocks of various size, churning up white froth. About a hundred yards upstream, a waterfall made a drop of about ten feet, sending up misty droplets that sparkled in the rising sun. Despite her desire to put Bo in his place, Lani couldn't help feeling tranquil and at ease in this idyllic setting.

"Here, get into these," Bo ordered and Lani turned to see him holding out a pair of chest-high rubber waders. His were already strapped over his shoulders. A giggle escaped from her throat.

"What's so funny?" he whispered.

"These boots," she replied, still giggling as she slipped them over her sneakers and jeans. "They make you look like a green penguin."

Bo rolled his eyes. Then he looked at her and snickered. "You look swell, too, Lani," he teased, looking at her equally ridiculous-looking waders.

He rigged both poles and, handing one to Lani, he moved gently into the stream. Lani waddled after him, starting to giggle once more until she slipped and nearly tumbled into the stream. Bo reached out a strong arm and easily pulled her to her feet.

"Careful, Lani, the bottom's very slippery. You may know your way around the advertising business, but out here I'm the boss, okay?" His face indicated he wouldn't take no for an answer and Lani merely nodded, afraid any sudden movement would send her tumbling into the water.

"Watch me, now. It's not hard." Bo fixed a miniscule, brightly decorated fly onto the end of the thick line and

## Conquering Embrace 119

proceeded to whip the end of the pole back and forth, back and forth. "The idea is to keep moving the pole while feeding out the line. That makes the fly or bait rise higher and higher until you've got enough line extended so you can cast out, feeding the line so that the fly glides through the air and lights on the water. We want the fish to think it's got a nice easy tidbit and snap it up."

Lani watched Bo go through the motions, his deft movements indicating his skill with the equipment. He tossed the fly out in a high arc and, just as he'd explained, it lit on the water with a little plop, sending out circular waves.

He quickly reeled it in and repeated the procedure. On the next toss, there was a splash around the fly, the rod tip dipped and Bo had hooked himself a beautiful, fighting trout.

Bo gently worked the fish in and, removing a net from his belt, scooped it up. To Lani's surprise, he talked gently, praising the fish for it's tenacity and character and then carefully put it back in the water and let it go free.

"Now it's your turn, Lani," he ordered.

She tried to imitate Bo's technique but after a few botched attempts and tangled line, all she could do was stand there, shaking her head in frustration. Bo sighed and waddled over to her.

"It's hard to get the hang of it at first. Here, let me give you a hand," he offered as he stepped up behind her.

Bo could've acted resentful of her earlier stubborn attempts to keep his mind on business but he seemed genuine in his efforts to teach her the rudiments of fly fishing. He stood behind her and placed his arms around her. His tanned cheek was a scant few inches from hers as he gripped the hand in which she held the rod.

"Relax your wrist, Lani. You want the rod to whip freely back and forth, that's it," he instructed, clearly enjoying being close to her.

Lani turned slightly to scan his rugged features, scrutinizing his obvious love of the forest. He was clearly in his element here in the woods but rather than take advantage of Lani's awkwardness, he chose to use the opportunity to get close to her, both physically and emotionally. "Come on now, Lani, keep your mind on what you're doing," he admonished teasingly after he caught her staring at him. He moved closer to her, taking her other hand and guiding it in the proper way to feed out line and make the cast.

His breath against the back of her neck made Lani shiver and lean back against his taut chest. She could tell by the huskiness in Bo's voice, as he coaxed her through the motions, that his desire was beginning to build also. But he stepped back and made Lani cast by herself. To her surprise, the fly shot far out over the stream and, much like Bo's had before, it plopped gently on the water. Bo was beaming his approval and Lani was feeling quite proud of herself when the line gave a sharp tug and started to stretch and dart across the stream.

"Whoa, you've got a big one, Lani. Easy, don't pull too hard. That's it, keep tension on the line..." Bo coached her evenly, and Lani was filled with the heady excitement of hooking a fish. Following Bo's instructions, she played the fish correctly, seeing the line move across the stream, away from her, making the reel sing as the fish dragged out more and more line. The vibrations of the tugging fish sent goosebumps over Lani's arms and she marveled at the fish's strength.

After about five minutes, she reeled it in and the fish, it's strength spent, was easily netted.

Lani could hardly contain her excitement as Bo gently unhooked the fish and held it before her in both hands.

It wasn't nearly as big as she expected but Bo seemed pleased with her effort nevertheless. "That's a fine rainbow trout, Lani. See how his sides reflect the colors?" he said as he moved the fish in the sunlight.

Lani gazed at the shimmering violet, blue, and pink

# Conquering Embrace

that reflected off the beautiful fish. "It's magnificent Bo. Shall we let this one go free, too?"

"He's yours, Lani, you decide," he answered, smiling warmly.

She nodded her assent, and Bo released the fish which swam away and disappeared beneath the rushing water. He turned toward her, his eyes gleaming, his tone softening. "You know, you don't look half bad in those waders; maybe you'll start a new fashion trend," he teased lightly.

Lani felt her cheeks flush and her heartbeat quicken. "How about some lunch?" he asked, taking her slender fingers in his hand and bringing them up to his lips.

"Sounds good to me," Lani replied, although she was only half thinking of food.

"Great. I've got some bread, imported cheese, a bottle of wine..." he continued, putting an arm around her shoulders and hugging her to him as they waded toward shore. But just before they reached the tangled root and leaf-covered bank, Bo started to slip, fought to regain his balance only to fall backwards into the stream, dragging Lani down with him. The stream was only a couple of feet deep but Lani shrieked as the icy cold water soaked her to the bone. She brushed wet strands of hair from her forehead as she saw Bo sitting up sputtering, pulling leaves out of his hair and shirt. The sight of the two of them, sitting in the stream was too much to bear and Lani broke into laughter, followed by Bo.

She was nearly in tears before she settled down and faced Bo. His eyes were now a deep brown, almost smoky, as he stared into her own blue eyes.

Lani's breath quickened as she moved closer to him. She tilted her head upward, focusing her eyes on the curving flair of his lips. Bo grasped the back of her neck and drew her toward him and she closed her eyes and gave him a warm kiss. Soaked and still sitting in the stream, Lani threw her arms around his neck, all her former anger gone, as Bo's tongue traced the soft inner lining of her mouth in a deliciously sensual exploration. She felt herself respond with increased passion before she considered their humorous situation.

"Oh, Bo," she gasped, pulling her mouth from his.

"Yes, darling," he murmured, his hands stroking her hair.

"Don't you think we should stand up and get out of this water?"

"I suppose so."

They started to get up but it was easier said than done. The waders were now filled with water and they had to struggle, slipping and falling again, before they were able to stand successfully.

Holding Bo's hand, Lani looked down at her waders and at Bo. The sight of them standing there with bloated waders was too funny to endure and Lani broke into a fit of laughter again as they waddled ashore. After they shed the waders, they scampered up the bank like two kids, to the spot where Bo had laid his pack. They continued unfastening their clothes and fell onto a patch of long grass. With their bodies nude and glistening in the warm, morning sun, they embraced each other hungrily.

All thoughts of her planned education for Bo fell by the wayside as Lani parted her lips and eagerly demanded his kiss. His muscled torso pressed heatedly against her goosebump-prickled flesh and Lani's heart raced.

"Oh, Lani, I knew that once we got away from the city, away from all that noise and confusion, it would be wonderful." His musky scent fired her deepest desires. His hands stroked and demanded a response.

Lani felt herself swirl toward total abandon as his mouth worked feverishly against her lips, her throat, and down to her nipples, coaxing them to stand in hard peaks against his soft, hot tongue.

"Oh, yes, darling, yes," Lani whimpered as she felt his heated strength rise and press against her. "I'm not all business, am I Bo? Tell me there's more, darling, tell

# Conquering Embrace

me," she demanded, running the tip of her tongue over the inside of his ear.

"You're nature's own child, Lani, now that I've got you away from civilization..." he replied huskily. Running a hand over her torso, Bo cupped a dark, swollen breast and stared fiercely into her aquamarine eyes, deep into her soul. "We've still got two whole days together, my love, let's make the most of them..." His voice dissolved into a series of low, animal-like groans as he drew himself into her.

A small cry escaped from deep within Lani's throat as she welcomed him with her own fiery desire. "Yes, Bo, that's it, oh, yes..." she trailed off as her senses crested and their rhythmic, athletic movements corresponded in this ultimate display of love. Whatever lay in store for Lani and her quarterback was an answer that was a world away. All that Lani cared about was the here and now. The sun continued to beam down, bathing their moving bodies in warm light as their fervor increased and Lani gasped, arching upward into the peak of her ecstasy...

# 9

LANI LOCKED THE Mustang and walked across the asphalt parking lot toward the entry gate of the Lions' practice field. The temperature must have been in the nineties. It was a sure sign that the late October Indian summer was underway. As her white espadrilles padded across the black surface, heat waves rippled the air and Lani wondered how on earth the team could stand such stiffling temperatures while dressed in their heavy pads and helmets.

Pausing to snatch a mouthful of water from a nearby drinking fountain, Lani reflected on the wonderful weekend in the mountains with Bo. In those brief two and a half days, she'd seen a side of him she hadn't expected. After they'd settled their differences, the mutual agreement they had reached had put their relationship in a whole new light. Despite her hard-nosed attempts to shape him into line, Bo had agreed to compromise and she had agreed to try looking at things from his point of view. She'd started out making her feelings about business and professional relationships perfectly clear. By the time the weekend had ended, Lani felt confident and satisfied about how she stacked up to Sheryl Canning in Bo's eyes. It wasn't much of a contest, Lani smugly surmised. Bo had simply been foolish to consider the offerings of that woman.

With their differences behind them, Lani and Bo had been able to experience the little vacation to the fullest. Bo had opened up a bit more about his past, revealing that he nurtured a basic sincerity derived from his love of nature. His musings about growing up in Kansas, spending many lazy afternoons hunting, fishing, learning about the wild, were something she could understand. The fact that he also worked hard on the family farm, while putting himself through school before he earned an athletic scholarship and was able to attend a major university, wasn't lost on Lani either.

The drive home was completely different from the drive up to the cabin. It was hard to drag herself away from such a wonderful experience. With everything between them out in the open, with her feelings and emotions exposed fully to him, there seemed to be no where to go but up. The news she came to give him today only seemed to confirm that their future would be everything she had dreamed it would.

Lani approached the practice field and saw the Lions going through their drills. And just like the last time she came to practice, Bo was wearing the only red jersey, leading one squad through a series of plays.

She took a seat in the nearly empty bleachers, at the side of the field, to wait for a break in the action when she could catch Bo. On the field, she focused on the linemen, snorting like bulls, their uniforms patchworks of dirt and grime, rips and ratty tape. The coaches taunted and goaded the players who crouched on their haunches, squaring off on either side of the line.

## Conquering Embrace 127

Even though Lani had seen the team practice before, and was familiar with the unique sounds that went along with it, when Bo signaled the center to hike the ball, the explosion of pads against pads and helmets against helmets that followed, was as startling as a thunder clap. The intensity of the initial hit between the two rows of linemen made Lani stiffen reflexively and put a hand to her throat. Even in practice uniforms, on a nondescript small college athletic field, the team in action was an impressive sight. With huge bodies storming everywhere, Bo sprang back agilely, before turning and lofting a short pass to a waiting halfback. With a ballet dancer's grace, the halfback tucked in the ball and started to pick his way downfield. But, despite their size, the men chasing him closed in quickly and leveled him like a grasshopper swatted down by a frisky tomcat.

Meanwhile, in the backfield, an overzealous defensive lineman steamed into Bo, sending him flying and the coaches into a fit of angry shouting. Bo went down hard and Lani winced and stood up anxiously. But Bo got up slowly, dusted himself off, and, with a pat on the helmet of the apologetic lineman, indicated he was okay.

Lani breathed a sigh of relief as one heavy-set coach proceeded to give the lineman a severe tongue-lashing.

As Bo led the offense on another play, Lani sat back down. "Your first time at a full contact scrimmage?" The masculine voice startled Lani and she turned to see a casually dressed young man, holding a note pad, sitting next to her. "Morely Stewart, *San Diego Herald*," he smiled, extending a hand.

"Hi! I didn't see you sit down," Lani replied, shaking his hand. "I've been to a practice before but it didn't seem this intense."

"It's not nearly as rough as it looks," he said. "The games are where the real action is."

"You could've fooled me," Lani replied. "I'm Lani Richards. Are you here to cover the team?"

"Yeah. This weeks' feature is about the veteran quarterback, with a slant on the team's chances of reaching the Super Bowl and whether or not this will be Cornell's last crack at the championship."

"I'd say that's a pretty fair bet," she commented.

"Sounds like you've got some inside info. You know Cornell?"

"Yes...I've made his acquaintance recently," she answered with a knowing smile.

"And how do you figure into all this, Miss Rich...Lani?" he asked, flipping open his pad.

Lani saw him readying his pencil and she hesitated a moment, wondering just how she should handle this.

"You're not seriously going to quote me, are you?" she asked, apprehensive.

"Maybe, depends on what you have to say," he replied matter of factly.

"I'm not sure I have that much to offer."

"Oh, come on, you wouldn't deny the press?" he smiled in reply, adding a wink for emphasis.

The young man's infectious smile got to Lani and she found herself smiling back, put at ease by his friendly manner. "Well, I've discussed Bo's intentions with him a couple of times and it's a real possibility that he'll leave football and embark on a media career at the conclusion of this season. But that's hardly big news, is it?"

"I don't know, it's not the first time I've heard that. Last year, he indicated he was going to retire, but after the Lions won the championship, Cornell didn't want to give up football. He came back for another season and so far the team's off to a good start. Who knows if he'll change his mind again," the man speculated.

The fact that Bo had already changed his mind about retiring once was news to Lani and she sat up straight facing the reporter directly. "Are you sure?"

"Yeah. I didn't cover the story myself but it was in all the sports pages. You know how these superstars are: It's in their blood. Some guys play until they're well into their forties. But most either lose their skills or get

# Conquering Embrace 129

beaten and bruised so much they fade out long before that."

It was a sobering revelation, and Lani felt her insides quiver nervously at the prospect that Bo fell into this same category. But he was different. He was sincere when he discussed his future plans, wasn't he? Lani wondered knitting her brow in confusion.

"Lani!" Bo's shout broke the momentary silence. She looked up to see the quarterback, helmet off, his face covered in perspiration, smiling at her from the nearby track that surrounded the field. He began to climb up the bleachers, his cleated shoes rattling on the wooden benches.

"Hello, Bo. Practice over?" Lani called, still nervous about what the sports writer had said.

"You kidding, those slave drivers haven't satisfied their lust for making us poor souls suffer. Just a little five-minute break. Hi, Morley, you trying to move in on my girl?" Bo joked, slapping the reporter affectionately on the back.

"The thought had crossed my mind, Bo," the reporter teased back.

"Well, forget it," Bo replied sitting beside Lani, giving her a light kiss on the cheek.

"You got a few minutes for an interview, Bo?"

"Sure, later though, okay, Morley?" Bo said, keeping his hazel eyes fixed on Lani.

"Thanks. I'll be around," the reporter replied before climbing down and hailing a nearby coach.

"I hadn't expected to see you here, Lani, but I can't say I'm not happy about it," Bo said, taking her hands lightly in his.

"It looked like you got tackled pretty hard. Are you okay, darling?" Lani asked, still pondering the reporter's words.

"Sometimes those rookies get a little over enthusiastic, but, yeah, I'm just fine... Takes more than that to ruin my day," he replied. Bo leaned back against the bench in the row behind them and put his feet up, taking a deep breath.

"How can you take all that punishment? I mean, it sounds like those guys are really hitting hard."

Bo turned his head and looked at Lani warily, as if gauging the extent of her concern.

"Sometimes they do," he began in a measured tone, "but it's not all that bad. Besides the little bit of punishment I take is worth it when I get the chance to really beat those giants with a long pass, or when I get this old body in gear and dazzle them with some fancy footwork." He laughed as he threw back his head and stared off into the bright sky.

He was obviously getting a kick out of the idea and Lani began to feel a pang of anxiety. Her fingers started trembling. "It sounds like you never really want to leave the game, Bo. That reporter said it's in your blood. Is that true?" she asked apprehensively.

"I suppose it is, but unless you've actually felt it, felt that exhilaration on the field, when the split-second timing is perfect, when all eleven guys are working in sync, you wouldn't be able to understand what it's all about."

The dreaded fear that Bo would place distance between Lani and his infatuation with football began to surface and, for just a moment, Lani was reminded of Ken and how he drifted away from her while pursuing a dream that ignored the physical realities that eventually limit all aging athletes.

"You forget I'm somewhat of an athlete myself, Bo. I know the thrill of winning. But I also know when it's time to give it up and concentrate on something more realistic," Lani said, fighting to keep the nervous edge out of her voice.

The look in Bo's eyes as he turned toward her revealed his annoyance. "What is this, a grilling?"

"I didn't mean it to sound that way, Bo... I'm just concerned, that's all. I don't want to see you get hurt,"

## Conquering Embrace 131

she offered, placing a hand behind his head and rubbing her thumb along the back of his neck.

"Oh, that feels good," he said, closing his eyes. "Don't worry about me, Lani. I've been at this a long time and I don't aim to be carried out on my shield, if you know what I mean."

"Cornell, you plan on getting back to practice or just heading off to a dance." Lani looked in the direction of the bellowing voice and saw a rawboned man standing in front of the bleachers, removing his baseball cap and scratching his head while he stared at Bo.

"Be with you in a minute, Jenkins," Bo yelled back.

*"Coach* Jenkins," the man fired back. "And don't be all day about it. I want you to run through that new flanker reverse pass," the man yelled as he turned and headed back toward the practice field.

"Duty calls," Bo said to Lani with a shrug of his shoulders.

"Sure Bo. Oh, I almost forgot, I've arranged for us to have dinner with the president of a men's sportswear company. I've just about convinced him you'd be perfect to plug his stuff but he's a Steelers fan and it looks like you'll have to charm him in person before he'll commit to anything. I've made a reservation at the restaurant for eight o'clock."

"I don't know, Lani," Bo replied hesitantly. "I've got to go over game films with the coaches. With the Houston game coming up, it's real important. If we win we'll be a shoe-in for the play-offs."

"But Bo, this could be a really big job, with national exposure. It could be all the difference in our plans," Lani responded, trying to control her mounting anxiety over Bo's seeming reluctance to accept the invitation. Did the team really practice all day only to work on plays and films the rest of the night? she asked herself.

Bo's features softened. "I suppose I can come straight from the evening meeting, if it's really that important."

"It is, Bo, believe me."

"I did promise to be more receptive to these affairs, didn't I?" He smiled, cupping her chin in his hand, staring affectionately into her blue eyes.

"Cornell!" the coach screamed from the distance.

Bo stood up and helped Lani to her feet. "I'll have somebody pick up a suit for me from my place. Don't worry..." he said, placing a gentle kiss on her lips and trotting down the bleachers.

"Call me at home later. I'll give you the details," Lani called after him.

The grunting, shouting and coaches' whistles faded in the background as Lani headed back to the Mustang. She'd thought Bo would have jumped at the chance to land a big job representing a major firm. His seeming indifference rekindled the memory of a similar experience.

Slipping into the bucket seat and starting the engine, Lani recalled her junior year in college. She and Ken were all set to drive down the coast of Baja California and spend a weekend in a remote Mexican fishing village. At the last minute Ken canceled out with a vague excuse about having to train that weekend for a special invitational track meet. Even though Lani was nearly in tears over the affair, she believed Ken. It wasn't until several weeks later that she'd learned Ken had skipped the track meet and spent that weekend partying with his buddies on the team. It took her a long time to figure it out, but when she understood why, she felt no better. To Ken his sport was more important than anyone and anything. And when he began to lose, his obsession wouldn't let him forget it. He simply couldn't feel comfortable with anyone but his compatriots on the field. He wasn't mature enough to deal with the other aspects of his life, even if it meant rejecting Lani.

Still miffed by the memory, Lani floored the accelerator and roared out of the parking lot. As she weaved her way through traffic, she wondered if Bo would follow the same pattern, once his body started to fail him, once he started to lose.

She pulled the car up to her condominium and hurried inside to get ready for the dinner meeting.

Sitting before the mirror at her dressing table, Lani opened the small straw box and gazed at the three black pearls nestled in a shiny satin handkerchief. She gently withdrew the precious little orbs from their home and held them in her hand, letting the light from the nearby table lamp shine over them. The pearls, fashioned into a pair of earrings and a matching pendant, were a gift from her grandfather. He had given them to her when she told him she was leaving the islands to move to the mainland, where she'd been accepted at the University of California at San Diego. She'd been reluctant to tell her white-haired mentor of her decision to leave her home on the big island, but it was something she had to do. To her surprise, he gave his blessing, recognizing that Lani was no longer a child but a budding woman, who, according to his infallible philosophy, should take the opportunity to move on and be a success in whatever she chose to do. He crowned his blessing with the little box and the then naked pearls. He'd dived for them himself as a boy and later gave them to his wife, Lani's grandmother. When the stately woman passed on, he saved them for Lani. She was almost afraid to accept such a precious gift, but the old man chuckled and proclaimed that they were things of beauty and a beautiful woman should be adorned with nature's greatest gifts.

Lani fixed the ear studs to her lobes and then threaded a thin gold chain through the matching gold setting on the pendant. She fastened the clasp at the back of her neck, letting the single pearl rest against the base of her throat, feeling her spirits lift as she stared at the exotic black pearls, as precious as any king's ransom. Even in her silky camisole, the effect was stunning. Lani sighed wistfully, surmising that nothing in her entire wardrobe could match the elegance of these little treasures.

She went to her antique armoire, throwing open the large wooden doors, wondering what to wear. Most of her clothes were either business formal or too casual; nothing she had would really show off the pearls as they should be. It was hopeless. She might as well go naked. Lani laughed out loud at the risque thought. That's certainly the way Bo would like it. Besides, the pearls contrasted wonderfully with her bare flesh. Yes, naked with just the pearls she'd look like a native straight from the forest. Lani shook her head, still smiling as she went through the rows of hangers in the closet.

A warm breeze gusted through the open bedroom window, blowing through Lani's thin camisole. The air felt good against her breasts and Lani felt her nipples harden in response. She would put all her fears behind her tonight, Lani decided. She would simply let nature take its course. Bo's charm and magnetic personality would probably woo the client just the way he wooed her on the set that first day. And whatever differences she had with Bo wouldn't enter their evening. More than anything else she just wanted to be with him, to feel his arms holding her.

The thin slated metal blinds began to bang against the window frame and Lani had just moved to close the window when the phone rang.

"Hello?"

"Lani, it's me," Bo said.

Something in his tone sent a chill through her.

"Something has come up and... well..."

"Bo, what is it, what's wrong?" Lani asked nervously, her hand starting to quiver slightly on the receiver.

"I can't make it tonight, darling. Sorry, but I'll make it up to you." His casual apology was like ice down Lani's back.

"But Bo, it's already been set up. You can't cancel out now. Don't you know what this means?" Lani asked, hardly believing her ears.

"I know this is important to you, darling, but..."

"Important to *me!* Bo, I thought we had an understanding. What happened to your sense of responsibility?" Lani interrupted, fighting for control. She wasn't prepared for Bo breaking their agreement and for a moment, she stood dumbfounded, silently holding the phone to her ear.

"Please, Lani, don't get upset," Bo continued. "I can't go into it now but believe me, I wouldn't break our engagement if it weren't for something important. You'll just have to try and understand."

"Understand! I understand all right. I thought you were an exception, Bo, but I guess I was wrong," Lani snapped, unable to control her rising anger.

"Exception to what?" he suddenly countered. "I'm not perfect and I don't fit a pattern, Lani. If you haven't figured that out by now you're in for a real shock."

"I'll say I'm shocked, Bo," she replied, slumping into the chair at her dressing table, unable to fathom the sudden change in her feelings for him. "I guess I was foolish to think you could settle down and begin to make a few simple commitments," she mused, half to herself.

"I meant what I said before, Lani, about trying to work by your rules. You'll just have to trust me, that's all."

"I think I know how much you can be trusted. It sure looks like I let myself get carried away by your smooth lines. But I know better now, Bo. What you're doing tonight is inexcusable. I think we've gone about as far as we can, don't you?" she asked, still hoping he would say something to ease her inner pain.

"I'll call you later," he said evenly.

"Why? Why bother?" she croaked hoarsely, fighting back the tears. "Good-bye, Bo..." she hung up the phone and nothing could have hurt Lani more. Just when everything seemed perfect...

Lani buried her face in her hands, feeling the sobs rising in her throat. She took several deep breaths trying to regain her composure. Through eyes blurred with tears, Lani watched herself in the mirror as she took off the pearls and placed them back in the box. The image quickly dissolved as the tears welled up and a solitary drop fell into the box and glistened as it slowly ran over the pendant.

Lani swallowed hard. How could she have been such a fool? How could she have let herself be taken in by another self-serving jock?

She clenched her hands into fists, digging her nails into her palms, until the physical pain began to clear her head. She could not afford to dwell on it. Feeling sorry for herself wouldn't help anything. What should I do? Lani asked herself, staring into the mirror. She needed to get out, to expel the tremendous reserve of nervous energy she'd built up. She needed her own private sanctuary.

Lani phoned the prospective client and canceled dinner. Then she grabbed her pink, halter-top maillot swimsuit, slipped it on and hopped into a bright purple, velour jogging suit. Picking up an extra-large bath towel and her keys, Lani hustled out the door, determined to forget the pain of Bo's unexpected betrayal.

# 10

LANI STRODE PURPOSEFULLY across the deserted sand toward the lightly pounding surf. She cast off the warm-up suit and tossed it down beside her towel. The onshore Santa Ana wind gusted hot over her skin and kicked up sand, pecking at her with stinging granules, making her feel alive. Despite the long shadows and approaching darkness, the temperature still had to be near ninety.

Lani bent low from the waist, stretching supplely, touching her toes, bending further, lightly putting her forehead against her knees. As she worked to loosen her muscles, she traced the definition of her legs. The maillot's high cut over the thighs enhanced the lean length of her legs and Lani liked the ultra-feminine effect.

Tossing her head, freeing her flowing dark chestnut locks, Lani sprinted toward the surf, feeling the shock as her legs churned through the icy, frothy residue of a retreating wave. Lifting her knees, she moved deeper and deeper until the water was at her waist. She stretched her arms overhead, arched, and dived into a swelling wave. With the air so warm, the cool water against her skin was a refreshing jolt. She kicked hard, holding her breath, plunging deeper, trying to get behind the rolling surf.

The chilling water was nearly pitch black. Lani stroked powerfully, through this silent underworld, straining her lungs to the limit, moving further and further offshore.

After what seemed like several minutes, when her lungs could stand no more, she darted for the surface. Like a breeching porpoise, Lani broke through, gasping loudly, sucking in a deep, satisfying breath, tossing the wet strands of her chestnut hair away from her face in a spray of flying droplets. Floating on her back, kicking her feet gently, Lani saw that she was about twenty or thirty yards from the beach. The exhilarating plunge had worked her muscles and raced her heart so that her blood was warming her skin despite the chilly temperature of the water. Feeling the swells of a mild sea lifting her floating body like flotsam, she gazed upward to the smattering of stars beginning to appear in the darkening sky. She shifted her gaze from one horizon to the other. Far out to sea the sun was an eerie, orange orb, seemingly resting on the blue-black water. Looking toward the shore, she saw the moon, just as large, beginning to rise majestically, shifting color from pale orange to pure white. Lani floated like a bobbing cork, between day and night, in a limbo between nature's most magnificent creations.

A splash nearby startled her and Lani turned to see the water rippling away in expanding circles from a spot behind her. After a moment, a pelican bobbed up to the surface, its gullet hanging full with a fish. The peculiar looking seabird pointed its bill upward, swallowed its catch, and flapped its expansive wings, lifting off the water and gliding upward as gracefully as any eagle.

In the distance, a mullet skipped over the water, set-

## Conquering Embrace 139

ting up a trail of splashes. The eerie phosphorescent quality of the sea on this moonlit evening made it seem as if Lani were in a different world. Removed from the bustling, fast-moving peopled world, she'd found a haven in this almost surreal place where seabirds, fish and all manner of other creatures pursued the more important matters of survival.

She kicked her feet gingerly, watching the flashing phosphorescent light from her splashes, illuminate her toes and her lean, slender legs. She toyed with the water, splashing with her hands, enjoying the light show and reveling in the delicious sensation of the frigid droplets cascading over her. Her skin was taut, bristling with goosebumps, every muscle firm. As her kicks propelled her further from shore, Lani gazed down the length of her supple body. She breathed deeply, watching the rise and fall of her breasts. Her thin nylon suit clung to her like a second skin. Fully wet, the tight, stretchy fabric was almost transparent and her aeroles were clearly visible, like dark, radiant coronas. Seeing her feminine charms so daringly revealed, Lani felt free, unhindered by earthly restrictions.

She began to surge with the feeling and inadvertently gulped a mouthful of salt water. It was harsh against her throat but Lani didn't care. It only served to remind her of her resolve to purge herself of the hurt of Bo's deceit.

After all that had passed between them, how could he have done this to her? How could she have been so wrong about him? How could he think she wouldn't be hurt when he treated her concerns so casually?

Lani's lips tightened as her anger flared again. Rolling onto her stomach, she stroked forcefully. Stretching out, reaching, Lani propelled her sleek body through the cool water. It streamed past her flanks as she began a rhythmic cadence of breathing, stroking, breathing, stroking. She angled her direction parallel to the shore and glided fifty yards, a hundred yards, a half mile. She tried to fight off the bitter memory by burning up her nervous energy, but her reserve of energy seemed boundless.

Nobody liked to admit they weren't as strong or as skilled as they were when they were young, Lani realized. Maybe retirement was too hard for Bo to come to grips with. And sports were a powerful potion that thrilled and intoxicated champions throughout history. The strongest of men had been driven to obsession in pursuit of sports glories.

Could she really expect any more from Bo? Wasn't it the spirit of the hunt that drove him to go beyond all reason in pursuit of such illusive goals. She'd simply expected too much of him. She'd ignored her own experiences in favor of her own desire. How gullible she'd been, how foolish, to think that he could be any different.

Lani stroked harder and harder, until the muscles in her arms and legs burned. But still her heart pounded in her chest. No one had made love to her like Bo. No one had sent shivers up and down her spine with a mere smile. When Bo stared at her with his penetrating hazel eyes, nothing matched the wave of desire that churned within her. And she loved him, damnit! Didn't he realize that? Didn't he care how much he was hurting her? Frustrated and angry, Lani forgot herself and swallowed another gulp of seawater, choking and sputtering.

She continued to swim for two hours, trying to find a solution to her pain. Slowly, her breathing eased. Her pulse, despite her growing fatigue, settled down and Lani finally began to relax. The swimming had burned off much of her nervous anxiety. She felt ready to leave the watery sanctuary and return to shore.

Lani casually swam toward shore, easing her heavily worked muscles, getting back into the pleasurable sensation of the soothing water. By now the moon was a third of the way up into the sky and the shore was bathed in its cool white light.

A lone figure was illuminated walking on the sand,

# Conquering Embrace

peering seaward. Definitely a man, Lani perceived. Straining to see in the soft light, Lani sensed something familiar in his manner. The figure paused and then began shedding his clothes. As he removed his shirt, his pants, his shoes, Lani caught a glimpse of his face, passing from shadow into moonlight. It was Bo. The image of his well-defined, trim body, gleaming in the moonlight, gripped her stomach in an icy fist. What was he doing here? How had he found her?

Lani watched incredulously as Bo jogged into the water and began swimming toward her. How dare he invade her private sanctuary, Lani wondered as her anger boiled.

His athletic body moved quickly through the water and Lani realized he was nearing her rapidly. Her blood began rushing hot and fast through her veins. She had to get away.

Twisting quickly, Lani sprinted off, stroking hard. But Bo was still closing the distance between them. Fueled by a rush of adrenaline, Lani's arms and legs worked like pistons, methodically driving her away. She risked a backward glance and saw that she was putting distance between them. Even though Bo was a magnificent athlete, few could match strokes with a woman who spent her childhood swimming as much as most people walked.

But Bo still kept coming. Lani turned and moved away again keeping him at a respectable distance. He still swam after her, stroking hard, pursuing her with an unbending resolve. What was he trying to prove? Lani asked herself. How long would he keep it up?

She couldn't help but admire the economy of his strokes. His splashes lit the water in phosphorescent flashes. His muscled torso, his well-formed calfs, his rippling shoulder muscles all gleamed and glistened. Lani felt goosebumps bristle up again as she riveted her gaze on his gliding form.

Should she make a dash for shore? She could probably beat him to the sand, she thought. But to what purpose?

Wouldn't it be better to stay and see what drove him so intrepidly to reach her? Knitting her brow in consternation, Lani argued with herself, trying to decide what to do. More than anything, she wanted to believe that Bo was the exception to her image of the spoiled, obsessed jock. Whether or not her hopes were realistic, she slowed her pace, allowing him to close the distance between them. She'd hear him out, find out what his intentions were. Lani could sense him gaining on her and her anxiety mounted. She heard his splashes growing louder, then his hand grasped her foot, halting her progress. Lani kicked at the hold he had on her, but his grip remained firm.

"Lani, stop. I'm not letting go," he yelled, breathing hard.

She relaxed and Bo grabbed her around the waist, turning her to face him.

"Your grandfather teach you to swim like that?" he asked, still breathing hard. "For a while there, I thought you might get away."

"Don't think I still can't," she answered, her voice tinged with hostility. "What do you want, Bo? What are you doing here?" she demanded, treading water beside him.

He looked hard at her, his hazel eyes flashing. Beads of water ran down his face, his jaw was set, firm, determined. "I couldn't let you go thinking something about me that wasn't true, Lani," he answered, breathing more evenly.

"I thought you'd made things perfectly clear," she replied calmly. "How did you find me anyway?"

"When you didn't answer your phone, I called your boss. He said you sometimes like to swim here, just south of the pier."

"Well, now that you've found me, what do you want?" Lani turned her head away from him.

He grabbed her wrist in one hand and her chin in the other. Pulling her toward him, turning her face to meet

## Conquering Embrace 143

his, he fixed her with a penetrating stare. "You've got me all wrong, Lani. Look at me!" he ordered as she squirmed in his grasp.

"You're hurting me, Bo," she replied angrily. She felt his grip relax but he still held her close.

"Lani, I meant what I said about meeting responsibilities. But you can't expect me to follow your dictates blindly, like a faithful dog. You've got to admit, this dinner engagement you arranged was on a pretty short notice." He was completely recovered from his exhausting swim and Lani felt his chest rise and fall evenly against her.

"I'll admit you didn't have much warning, but that's how it is in this business sometimes. I didn't think you'd be put out by it," she said sarcastically.

"Listen to yourself, Lani. It's clear from your tone that you've already judged and sentenced me without hearing my side of things."

"I think I've heard plenty and so far none of it makes me feel any better."

She saw his features soften and he let her wrist go. "I know I owe you a better explanation than the few words we had over the phone. Lani, when you left my practice session this afternoon, I thought everything was just perfect with us. I even sent the team manager over to my place to grab some clothes, just like I said I would. The team was running through a new play just before we quit for the day and then wham, my knee... I wasn't hit or anything. It just seemed to catch fire and the next thing I knew I was on the ground. The pain subsided, but I was still worried that I might've injured myself severely."

"Bo are you okay? How serious is it?" she asked nervously, unable to contain her concern.

"I'm not sure really. It's an old injury from my rookie year. I twisted it up pretty good back then and every now and then it acts up, but nothing like this afternoon."

"Why didn't you tell me, Bo, I would've understood."

"I didn't want to worry you without reason, Lani. These things aren't always what they seem. I had to see a doctor, a specialist in athletic injuries. I couldn't wait. I had to know whether I'd be playing Sunday or laying on an operating table waiting to have my future determined by a surgeon. I *had* to break that dinner engagement. I had to get my knee examined and hear the verdict." He searched her eyes as he continued, "So far, it looks okay. I can play Sunday."

She hoped that he was telling the truth, that the injury wasn't that serious. But whether he was injured or not, the fact that something that happened on the field had kept him away from her continued to eat away at Lani. "Bo, how much longer do you think you can keep it up? Do you really expect me to believe something so painful could really be all right just like that?"

"Why do you always want to believe the worst about me, Lani?" he demanded, his eyes narrowed to slits. But Lani remained firm in her resolve to get the truth out of him. After a moment's standoff, he relaxed and sighed loudly, "Okay... my knee's not perfect but the injury is such that I'll be able to manage for a while yet. There're some cartilage splinters floating around in the joint and they've got to come out eventually, but surgery can wait until the end of the season. As for the pain, it comes and goes. I can live with it. Right now, I don't feel a thing... at least in my knee," he said pointedly, obviously losing patience with her.

"That's great, Bo. I fall for a guy who doesn't think he can trust me enough to share something that matters to both of us. And worst of all, you act like nothing's wrong, without a second thought that you could lose the use of your knee, maybe forever."

"I suppose I should have confided in you earlier," he admitted.

But Lani was still angry and couldn't let the matter go. "What kind of future do we have if you continue to abuse your body to the point of becoming lame just

## Conquering Embrace    145

because of your obsession with a kid's game? How many times will I get calls that you've been rushed to the hospital, or that you can't meet a business obligation because you're being patched up so you can play the next Sunday and the next and the next? How many Sundays will there be, Bo? I can't... I won't take a back seat to a football game, no matter how precious it is to you," she shouted with finality.

"Damnit, Lani, listen to me," he shouted back, his voice hot with anger. "You'll never take a back seat with me, ever! I love you, Lani, and nothing can change that. You've got me so hung up I can't even remember our plays half the time. You talk about our future... Darling, I can't even get through a single day without wanting you in my arms, smelling your hair, feeling your body against me."

The words hit Lani hard and she felt her resolve melt under his intensity. She wanted desperately to believe him. "Bo... I love you, too. You're all I think about anymore, but I'm just not sure I can handle the thought of losing you every autumn while you press your luck fighting father time." Lani's bottom lip began to quiver as she tried to find the right words to express how deeply she felt for him.

"Lani, this is it for me, my final season. I'm retiring from football."

Lani arched her eyebrows and she stared deep into his hazel eyes. The words reached out and grabbed her very soul.

"Believe it, darling," he continued. "We've got a lot of things to do together and the sooner we get to them, the better." His lips stretched into a warm, beaming smile and Lani could no longer contain her joy. The corners of her mouth spread into a warm smile of her own.

"I do want to believe it, Bo, more than anything in the world," she replied, her eyes misting over in happiness.

"All I ask is that you bear with me until the season

is over," he said, his eyes crinkling as his smile broadened. "It takes a lot of concentration and nearly all my energy to prepare for these last games. We can make the play-offs and if we get any kind of luck at all, we can be back in the Super Bowl. Afterwards, it'll all be over and behind me. But for now, I need you to be patient. Things will get real intense the next few weeks and you'll probably think I'm a walking zombie when you see how psyched-up I can get for the games. The pressure is tremendous, but it's what I get paid for."

There were only a couple of months to go, Lani realized. Despite her apprehensions and concern for Bo's safety, it wasn't a long time to wait. It could mean all the difference. "I guess I can manage it, Bo; it's not that long," she replied, lowering her long eyelashes, sure she'd gush out her joy should she look at him directly.

"How long do you think we can keep treading water like this?" he asked jokingly, his breathing becoming labored.

"I can probably stay out here all night," Lani teased, as she realized she was growing tired herself.

Bo snaked a hand through the water and reached for her waist, pulling her toward him. "You're quite a mermaid, aren't you," he whispered huskily as their legs moved and intertwined in the water. As his chest rose and fell against her, Lani felt Bo's chest hair through the thin fabric of her suit and, as it brushed across her nipples, shudders coursed through her. His body heat radiated over her, warming her against the cool water. Lani ran her hands down his back, tracing his muscles, stroking downward. Her hand continued over bare flesh, over the swell of his firm, hard backside and Lani gasped in surprise. He was naked!

"Are you crazy, Bo, this is a public beach?" she teased, giggling.

He smiled back rakishly. "Who cares? All I know is that I want you Lani, your body thrills me like nothing else." His nostrils flaired slightly and his mouth descended on hers. She tasted the salt on his lips and felt herself responding, quickly finding his tongue with her own.

Bo pressed himself against her and Lani could feel his heat surging. Suddenly her feet bumped something and she looked toward shore, "All this time we were talking we've drifted in," she realized out loud.

"Tide's coming in," he acknowledged.

An incoming swell lifted them up and carried them both further in toward the beach. As the backwash from the wave subsided, it left them in water down to their waists. Lani stared at the water running off Bo, down his chest, following a trail past his navel, meeting the water where his waist funneled down to his hips. His well-developed body was godlike, glistening in the moonlight. Lani's heart pounded, and a spark flickered and caught fire within her loins. She ran her gaze upward, settling on his full, flairing lips. He broke into a wicked grin.

Lani traced his stare and realized the wet fabric of her suit was revealing all her feminine charms. Her breasts showed firm and full through the tight nylon. Bo raked his eyes over her in a quick, fluid move. He inhaled deeply and drew her toward him. "That's almost no suit at all," he breathed hotly against her cheek, reaching a hand around her neck.

"It's a racing suit, the form-fitting nylon makes me more efficient in the water, cuts down on drag," she replied dreamily, grazing her lips over the hollow between his neck and jaw. She tasted his salty flesh and flicked her tongue under his earlobe.

A low groan escaped from Bo's throat as he unfastened the strap at the back of her neck. Still pressed tightly against her, Bo tugged and pulled the top of her suit down to her hips. The transition from nylon against flesh to flesh against bare flesh was a delicious thrill and Lani shivered with pleasure.

A foghorn bellowed eerily in the distance and voices

filtered softly from the nearby pier. A wave washed over them pushing Lani closer to Bo. The water flowed off their shoulders and she shivered again as her cool, wet flesh was met by the hot desert breeze from shore.

"I could take you right here, Lani," he said, his voice thick with desire. "Your skin, so firm, so hot." He moaned, running his hand down her back, along her curving hips, cupping her backside, and pressing her tightly against his powerful thighs.

Lani closed her eyes and lifted her feet, languishing in his sensual grasp, allowing him to guide her body, nearly weightless in the rising and falling water. But the voices on the pier cut through the passionate mist and Lani pulled back slightly, murmuring through half-closed eyes, "Bo this is crazy. There're too many people around. What if someone sees us?"

Still holding her close, he shifted his gaze and broke into a conspiratorial smile. "I guess you're right. Besides, my reputation is tarnished enough; a scandal like this could really keep me out of doing commercials." He laughed heartily at his joke.

Lani giggled back and pushed away from his chest, pulling up the top of her bathing suit.

"Let's go back to my place," he suggested, running a hand through the wet strands of her hair, leaving no doubt about his building desire.

"Ummm," Lani replied and dashed up the beach. She grabbed her towel and started to work it over her hair when she saw Bo standing beside her, dripping wet, nude and wonderful. A trio of boisterous teenagers scampered over the sand nearby and Bo furrowed his eyebrows, looking helpless, as he seemed to consider putting on his trousers while still wet. Lani couldn't help laughing at him and tossed him her towel. As she stepped into her jogging suit, he rubbed himself dry and pulled on his trousers, smiling suggestively.

"Follow my truck. We've still got some things to settle," he said as his lips curled into a seductive smile.

## Conquering Embrace 149

Hand in hand they padded across the sand, the hot breeze quickly drying their hair, clearing their senses. Lani's previous anxiety was gone. Now her heart beat with the anticipation of fulfilling her need for the man she loved.

# 11

"I WON'T DO it, it tastes terrible," the little girl bellowed and ran off the set in tears, into the waiting arms of her mother.

"Holy smokes!" George exploded in frustration, "now what am I supposed to do?"

Lani tossed down her notes and walked across the set to the perturbed director. "George, why don't we break for about ten," she offered, placing an assuring hand on his shoulder. "We could all use the rest. Everybody's getting jumpy."

"Sure... why not? We're already two hours into overtime and half the crew's screaming to get home and watch the football play-offs on TV..." he moaned, half to himself.

What a day! After ten hours of trying to shoot a simple breakfast food commercial, they were no further along than when they started. And she couldn't blame the five-year-old girl for getting fed up. Lani probably would have felt the same way if she'd had to sit under those hot lights all day, hearing George's instructions become frantic as the day grew longer. The poor little thing must have eaten four or five bowls of the cereal. She was probably stuffed.

"Larry," Lani called, searching for the normally exuberant gofer.

"Yeah, what do you need, Miss Richards?" the shaggy haired twenty year old managed in a tired voice.

"See if you can come up with a shot of whiskey for George. I know there's some around here somewhere."

"Sure thing," he replied and walked off.

Normally, she didn't allow any drinking on the set until they were through shooting, but this had been an ordeal and anything to counteract the effects of the long day and settle the director down was welcome.

She turned and walked back to George. "I'll talk to the child, don't worry. We'll get this thing wrapped up tonight. Meanwhile, you sit down and take a few deep breaths or something, okay?" Lani calmly suggested, trying to ease the tension that had built up during the last couple of hours.

"Here you go, Miss Richards," Larry interjected, holding out a paper cup filled with ice and brown liquid.

"Thanks," she said taking it and holding it out to George. "Take a slug of this, George."

He eyed the offering suspiciously, smelled it, and took a tentative sip. "Scotch!"

"Best I could do," Larry answered with a smile and a shrug, "but it's the good stuff, twenty dollars a bottle."

"Thanks, kid," George replied, settling down into a canvas director's chair and casting a bemused look at Lani.

She returned a tired smile and headed off in search of the child actress. It seemed that everything that could go wrong did. First, the power went out when the strong winds outside toppled a power pole. Next, the tape re-

# Conquering Embrace 153

corder broke down and, as if things weren't going badly enough already, the caterers phoned in saying their truck blew a tire on the freeway and lunch would be late.

It seemed like this was the norm, however, and during the last couple of weeks things continued to grow more and more hectic. Still, Lani welcomed the diversion, however much her tired feet ached and her eyelids drooped from fatigue. In the month and a half since that night on the beach with Bo, she'd buried herself in her work, hoping to make the time fly as quickly as possible. He'd asked her to be patient for a couple of months while his team tried to make the play-offs and get into the Super Bowl. With the big game a mere two weeks off, Lani felt her diligence paying off. Just let me get through these next two weeks, Lani prayed, and everything would be all right.

She sighed wistfully, remembering how wonderful everything had turned out that night. They'd gone back to Bo's house and spent the rest of the evening in bed. Even now, the memory of their heated lovemaking warmed her insides. In the weeks since, they'd only been together twice, but Bo's phone calls filled the gaps and, even though he grew increasingly preoccupied with the championship game, his voice soothed and filled her with anticipation of the wonderful times that lay ahead of them. Her fears that he would be reluctant to leave football at the end of the season surfaced occasionally, but she fought to push them aside, choosing to dwell instead on Bo's promise and the growing excitement she felt as the season drew to a close. She'd been patient and it would all work out. It had to, because without Bo in her life, Lani would surely be a wreck.

She reached the dressing room and, after a little knock on the door, she poked her head inside. "Jennifer, Jenny?" Lani called as she saw the cherub-faced little brunette snuggled in her mother's arms.

"Say hello to Miss Richards," her mother coaxed, and Jenny lifted her head.

"Hello..." she said in a tired voice.

"Please come in Miss Richards," the mother offered, and Lani entered and sat on the little couch beside them.

"You're not gonna make me eat any more of that junk, are you?" Jenny pleaded in a cranky voice.

Lani laughed and placed a gentle hand on the girl's forehead. "Is it really that bad?"

"It's awful and the milk's all warm, yucch!" She answered, sticking out her tongue for emphasis, while her mother just looked toward the ceiling, sighing loudly, her own frustration from the long day in evidence.

"Well, we'll just have to do something about that, won't we?" Lani assured Jenny. "I'm sure we can get it right and over with. Jenny, what would make that terrible old cereal better?" Lani asked, smiling at the little girl, hoping for a suggestion.

Jenny screwed up her face trying to think of something, "How about chocolate?" she blurted, serious.

"Jenny!" her mother scolded. "That sounds terrible."

"What about some kind of fruit, Jenny? How does that sound?" Lani asked, still laughing at the girl's suggestion.

Jenny hesitated and her mother chimed in, "You like strawberries don't you, honey? How about if Miss Richards gets you some strawberries to put on the cereal?"

"Chocolate strawberries?" Jenny asked hopefully.

"How about the strawberries first and the chocolate afterwards, that is if your mom doesn't mind," Lani suggested, looking from Jenny to her mother.

"Well...all right, I guess so, but I'd really like to finish this soon, okay?"

On seeing Jenny's mother's consenting nod, Lani stroked Jenny's cheek with the back of her hand. "I'll get George to make sure everything goes as smooth as possible, I promise. Do we have a deal?" Lani asked, holding out her hand.

"Okay, a deal," Jenny replied, taking Lani's hand in her own tiny one and shaking vigorously.

## Conquering Embrace 155

"Say thank you to Miss Richards, Jenny," her mother reminded her.

"Lani," the ad executive offered.

"Thank you, Lani," Jenny replied and stood up, shaking out the wrinkles from her jumper, brushing her dark brown locks aside, and, like a trooper, she said, "Okay, I'm ready, let's get it over with."

Lani laughed and yelled for Larry to run out for some strawberries and the best chocolate he could find.

After all the turmoil and chaos, they wrapped up the shoot in just an hour. With a collective sigh of relief, the crew straggled off and Lani drove back to her office.

Absentmindedly, Lani popped one of Jenny's cherry-filled chocolate candies into her mouth as she rode the elevator up to her office. Even though it was well after hours, she wanted to take care of some unfinished work on her desk before heading home.

Once again she reflected on being with Bo after he retired, the things they could do, the places they could go. The time couldn't pass fast enough for Lani.

She reached her office, only to be confronted with a desk piled high with yet to be read scripts. Joyce was long gone, but she'd left a list of phone calls Lani had received while she was working on the sound stage. One stood out from all the rest. Bo had called but left no message.

Smiling, Lani reached for her phone and dialed Bo's number. His phone rang but went unanswered. Lani hung up vowing to try later.

Two memos and an hour later, Lani stuffed several script proposals for one-minute commercials into her leather bag and switched off her desk lamp. She strolled through the reception area when she heard loud, male voices coming from Charlie's office. Shifting her direction, she walked up to his office door.

No sooner had she gripped the doorknob than a vocal roar erupted from inside. Poking her head in, Lani saw Charlie, Jeffrey, the staff art director, Pete and the company lawyer, Roger, in various poses of recline around a small color TV set, watching a pro football game.

"Lani, find someplace to sit and get yourself a drink," Roger called before returning his eyes to the set.

"Did you see how he got away from *three* tacklers. That's the prettiest run I've seen all year," Charlie exclaimed, sipping on a highball and munching a handful of peanuts.

Pete extended a piece of paper to Lani. It was divided into a series of squares with numbers on the edges of them. In several of the squares were the written names of various company staff members. "Office pool, Lani, you want in?"

"Don't tell me you guys are in here gambling?" she teased.

"Sure, it's the American way. Makes the game more interesting," Charlie remarked. "It's ten bucks a square, if you're so inclined," he added with his eyes glued to the screen.

Before she could reply the guys erupted into another chorus of excited cheers. Shaking her head, Lani gazed at the television set. During the last couple of weeks practically the whole town had become caught up in the play-offs. Everywhere she went, Lani realized, somebody was stationed before a TV or radio, taking in the onslaught of play-off games that suddenly poured over the airwaves. Everybody was football crazy.

"I'll find another way to throw away my hard earned pay," she finally answered, watching the action on the screen.

"Where's your spirit of adventure, Lani?" Roger teased while grabbing a frosty can of imported beer from a compact refrigerator in the corner.

She put down her briefcase and took the can from him. After popping it open, Lani looked around and, finding a glass, she poured her beer into it. No matter how much she appreciated her fellow associates treating her like one of the guys, she wasn't about to drink from

## Conquering Embrace    157

the can. She took a chair and pulled it up to complete the huddle around the TV.

"Bet she doesn't even know who's playing," Roger said to no one in particular.

"Sure I do, Mr. Macho football fan," Lani countered, "Pittsburgh, Dallas, semi-finals, winner plays the Lions in the Super Bowl." She took a sip of the cold beer. The slightly bitter liquid slid refreshingly down her throat and the carbonation quickly sent up a slight burp. She tried to suppress it but the guys heard nevertheless and exchanged chuckles.

Despite her long day Lani welcomed the chance to relax with her coworkers and, slipping off her shoes, she stared at the game on the flickering tube.

A time-out was called and, as the program shifted to a commercial, Charlie turned to Lani, with a leering smile. "You know, guys, Lani's not as ignorant of the game as you might think. I know she's got the inside line on the Lions and on their star quarterback in particular."

She felt her face flush in response to Charlie's reference to her involvement with Bo. "I may know a thing or two," she conceded, trying not to let him enjoy her embarrassment.

Pete swiveled around in his chair. "I'm planning on putting a bundle down on the Lions, Lani, any chance you can use your remarkable talents to give Cornell that little something extra?" he hinted with a sly wink.

"You guys," Lani breathed in mock exasperation. "Since you're betting a bundle, maybe I'll convince Bo to throw the game, how's that?" she stated, trying to get his goat.

"Bo, is it?" Jeffrey asked, doing his best to drawl out the innuendo.

"Now, now," Charlie cajoled, "no need to tease Lani about her own private business. Let's just enjoy the little glow that seems to be lighting her face now that she's trying to get him involved in the company. Haven't you noticed how hard she's working now and how little she complains?" he suggested, trying hard to keep from laughing.

Lani had to keep her face toward the screen. She knew Charlie would read her like a book and only laugh harder. "It's good to know my hard work doesn't go unnoticed. I expect a handsome bonus for my efforts, whether or not the Lions win the Super Bowl," she finally countered, trying to sound smug about it. After a moment, they all broke up in laughter.

Despite their delight in teasing her, Lani found herself feeling at ease talking about Bo and actually began to get involved with the men as they followed the play by play with a series of running comments. Perfect armchair quarterbacks, she mused, while studying the game on the screen.

It went on like that until half-time. After a series of commercials and a recap of the first half, the program shifted to a prerecorded interview with the Lions players on the practice field. Lani was thinking of heading home when the reporter began to interview Bo.

Lani's attention was drawn back to the screen. There was Bo, his hair now long enough to hang down over his forehead, where it clung, wet with perspiration. Bo, in his pads, seemed to tower over the reporter like a gladiator taking a break from the arena. His flashing smile and rugged features, covered with his sweat, made him as appealing as ever. Lani smiled inwardly, proud of the fact that indeed, she did have the inside track with the Lions' star.

The interview began with the usual questions about the Lions chances in the Super Bowl and how they matched up against the two teams competing for the chance to meet the Lions for the championship.

Bo was as cool as ever before the camera and Charlie commented on the great job Lani was doing in directing him toward their agency. But Charlie's comment was suddenly eclipsed by a poignant question from the re-

## Conquering Embrace 159

porter. He mentioned Bo's recent flair-up of injuries and the fact that now, after the Lions have already won two championships, maybe their aging quarterback had lost the edge.

Lani cocked her ears toward the screen.

"Injuries are a part of the game," Bo answered matter of factly. "But I feel good, ready to play."

"I'm sure that's good news for San Diego fans," the reporter commented. "But seriously, Bo, after some fifteen years in the league, isn't it just a little bit harder to keep going, to find the motivation to get out there on the field, taking the punishment year after year?"

"Sure, and those defensive linemen seem to get bigger and meaner every year," Bo joked. He continued, this time his tone more serious, "Once I get into a game, though, I forget about everything but executing, scoring, winning. And right now, nothing looks as sweet to me as winning that third Super Bowl."

"There's been a lot of talk about you calling it a career after this season, Bo, what's the story on that?"

Bo broke into a broad grin, "Everybody's got to give in to their age sooner or later but I'll tell you straight, Bryant, I intend to go out a winner."

"With both Pittsburgh and Dallas featuring hot young quarterbacks and solid defenses, you'll have your work cut out for you."

"They're both good teams, Bryant, anytime you get into the Super Bowl you've got to be a good team. But like I said, I don't aim to lose and I don't aim to leave the game of football as a loser," Bo confirmed with intensity.

Lani stared at the television dumbfounded. It felt like someone had slammed a fist into her stomach. As she stared at Bo in disbelief, he seemed to be possessed with a fervor, as if his mind were a million miles away from his retirement plans. As if he didn't intend to ever retire. The small talk among her colleagues was a far off din. Lani looked at the screen as if in a trance.

"Then there's a chance we'll see Bo Cornell again next year?" the reporter hinted.

"Could be ... but I'm not thinking that far ahead, I'm just looking to play them one at a time and the next one is where all my energy is going," Bo said soberly, folding his arms across his chest.

The reporter turned toward the screen as Bo moved off. "Well, you've heard it from the horse's mouth," the reporter summed up for the TV audience. "Lions' quarterback Bo Cornell could be winding up his career here in San Diego, if he can pull in another championship. But that's a mighty big *if* and, as he suggested, the oldest pro quarterback playing today since George Blanda started for the Raiders a decade ago, may be back for another season or two. From San Diego, this is Bryant Miller."

The program shifted back to the play by play announcers and the second half got underway. But Lani had seen enough. Charlie's office seemed hot and stiffling. She had to get out of there. How could Bo have changed his mind? Or did he change it? Maybe he never seriously considered retiring at all. Lani's head whirled with the rash of questions.

All her well-ordered plans for Bo's retirement suddenly seemed to wash away. Lani hastily excused herself, picked up her bag, and headed for the elevators.

As she watched the row of numbers light up, indicating the elevator was rising up to her floor, Lani ran a palm over her brow, wiping away the beads of perspiration, trying to regain her composure. Perhaps Bo was merely caught up in the excitement that went along with preparing for the big game. She knew from her college tennis days that athletes sometimes went through intense periods of concentration, where they literally psyched themselves into an acute state of readiness, like a stretched-out rubber band, straining to snap back and expend the stored up energy. Maybe Bo's comments were the result of such a preoccupation with the Super Bowl. A butterfly fluttered nervously inside her as she hoped desperately that what Bo said during the TV interview did not really reflect on the intimate words he'd shared with her.

The marker for her floor lit up and the elevator doors opened. Lani stepped inside, staring at her shoes, still trying to puzzle out what she'd heard on the television. The elevator car quickly reached the lobby and the doors opened.

"That's what I call great timing," the familiar voice announced.

Lani looked up to see Bo, framed in the elevator doorway, smiling lazily at her.

With the TV interview burning in her mind Lani had to fight the urge to blurt out her anxieties to him. "Bo... I got the message that you called..." she replied, searching his smiling features for a clue of his feelings, wondering if he'd mention the interview.

"Right, this is my last night in town before the team flies to San Francisco for the Super Bowl. I thought you might like to go out for a drink, maybe dinner, before I say good-bye for the next two weeks." Without waiting for an answer, he took her arm and led her out of the elevator, toward the parking lot.

"Mr. A's okay?" he asked as they reached his truck.

"Sure, Bo," she replied. "But what about my car?" Lani asked as he held the passenger door of the truck open for her.

"We'll pick it up later... in the morning," he replied with a roguish grin.

Lani climbed into the cab and Bo closed the door with a resounding bang. As he took his seat behind the wheel and started the engine, Lani considered Bo's unexpected arrival, deciding it was just what she needed. Over a drink and dinner, far removed from any practice field, Bo might reveal exactly what he meant by his response to the reporter's question.

It wasn't long before traffic piled up and the truck was stuck in a major rush hour jam. To make matters worse, the temperature was still in the upper eighties. Lani rolled down her window but the stench of exhaust fumes, coupled with the heat and noise of idling engines and honking drivers, was nerve wracking. They were near the airport and a huge passenger jet roared overhead, drowning out the traffic hubbub in an overpowering combination of noise and vibration.

Lani rolled her window up, preferring the heat to the noise and smells outside.

"Sorry there's no air conditioning in here. It's one of the little options I didn't care about at the time I bought this rig," he offered apologetically as he switched on the radio. He quickly tuned in to the last minutes of the football playoff game.

The truck was filled with a new cacophony, hardly preferable to the din outside. As the announcers called the action, Lani watched Bo's features react. His brow knit, then relaxed, his smile tightened, disappeared, and then came back as he responded to a call he liked.

"I guess this time of year your thoughts really do get wrapped up in the play-offs," Lani commented in response to Bo's reactions.

"Yeah, the whole season boils down to these last few weeks. Sorry I haven't been able to spend more time with you, Lani... but I did warn you." He offered a placating smile.

Lani nodded, forcing a small smile, still feeling the nagging tug at her insides over Bo's words on the television.

"Oh, almost forgot, here," he said, producing two tickets from his jacket pocket and holding them out to her.

Lani took them and looked dully at the words printed on their faces proclaiming seat and aisle locations for the San Francisco Super Bowl, featuring San Diego and the winner of the Dallas–Pittsburgh game.

He moved the truck forward a scant few yards before the traffic halted again. Lani continued to stare at the

## Conquering Embrace 163

tickets when he said, "Well c'mon, Lani, don't you care to come to the big game and root for your champion?" he asked, annoyed at her lack of enthusiasm.

"Uh, sure, Bo... it's just that..." Lani fought to find the right way of expressing her anxiety and she saw Bo's eyes search her face, aware of something amiss.

"What is it, Lani? I can tell something's up with you."

"Bo, I saw you being interviewed on TV, during the half-time show for this game," she began in a measured tone.

But his mind had suddenly shifted back to the game on the radio and he drowned out her words with a loud comment on a play.

"Bo..." she began unable to hide the rising note of anger straining her voice. But he held up a hand to try and silence her while he concentrated again on the play from the radio.

Suddenly, as if the building pressure had strained her dam of patience to the limit, Lani felt her anger rise to the bursting point. "Bo, listen to me!" she snapped, clicking off the radio.

He turned to her with a start, his features reflecting his surprise.

"You said in the TV interview that unless you won the Super Bowl, you'd play again next year," she continued, trying to keep her voice from cracking.

He raised a thick eyebrow and fixed her with an intense hazel stare. "Are you sure, Lani? I don't think that's exactly what I said," he answered tentatively.

"I'm sure. You may not have used just those words but there wasn't any doubt about your intentions to play until you won another Super Bowl. What about your promise to me?"

"Lani, I thought this matter was all settled. Didn't we decide to let things go until the season ended. You agreed to give me two months, remember?" he replied, his voice beginning to take on a note of impatience.

"Sure, I remember. I also remember you saying that

after this season was over, I'd never have to take a back seat to the game again. Do you remember that, Bo?" she asked, biting her lower lip in vexation.

"You'll always be first on my list, darling," he answered and reached out a hand to gently cup her chin. "It's just that this is a difficult time now. I've got a big challenge coming up, a big responsibility. I know you deserve more attention than you've been getting lately, but I can't afford to worry about anything else but the championship. You can understand that can't you?"

Lani swallowed hard against the lump rising in her throat and turned away from him, staring out the side window. "I guess...I guess I'd hoped for too much," she said absently to herself. "Once a jock, always a jock. You'll never give it up, Bo, at least not until you've wrecked your knees, or wound up on the ex-quarterback junkpile," she reflected bitterly.

He reached over and gently grasped her shoulder, turning Lani to face him. His eyes danced in sparkling amusement.

"It's not that bad, darling..." he offered in a soothing tone, but something about his condescending manner only served to eat deeper into her heart. "There's still a little life left in these old bones...you'll see, Lani, we'll win this game, I'll survive and it'll be just you and me, free to do whatever we want."

Lani was unable to believe he actually cared for her concerns. He was like a little boy, lost in a fantasy world, where life's solutions hinged on the outcome of a football game. His unbending confidence about winning the game and their troubles being over only frustrated her more.

"Let's put this behind us, Lani. I need you in the stands cheering me on," he coaxed reaching for the radio dial.

"Cheerleading's not my style, Bo," she replied coldy. "I can't follow after you, applauding what happens on the field when at any moment you could be hurt and everything I've hoped for could be destroyed in an instant."

"Nonsense," he answered, switching the radio on again. "With all the publicity this game will generate for me, for *us,* my celebrity status will be ensured for the rest of my life, Lani."

Lani could hardly believe her ears. The heat in the truck mounted and she rolled the window down again, preferring the noise and smog to the smothering confines of the truck. Bo's dreams of glory, while totally ignoring her concerns, made her numb. Images of Bo wincing with pain in the jacuzzi, or raucous fans bloodthirstily goading him on, of those same fans laughing at an overaged, hobbled quarterback, still trying to compete with a generation of younger, stronger, faster behemoths, flooded her mind.

She looked at Bo and realized he was in a world all his own. He was oblivious to her rising grief. She suddenly couldn't stand him sitting there listening to the game on the radio.

Lani's vision blurred as the tears welled up in her eyes. It couldn't go on. Bo was lost to her and all her dreams of an idyllic life with him after he retired seemed washed away like the sands of a beach pummeled by an unrelenting surf.

Turning back to Bo she held out the tickets. "Good luck, Bo . . ." she said nervously.

"What?" he replied, gazing at the tickets she held in front of him.

The heat and noise had finally pumped her anxiety to the limit. On the verge of tears Lani saw that traffic was barely moving and grabbed the door handle.

"Lani, wait a minute . . ." he said as she lifted the door handle.

To her relief, the door opened this time. Lani dropped the tickets onto the dashboard and stepped out into the street. She slammed the door behind her and, fighting the urge to look back, dashed for the curb.

Overhead, black smoke from a distant brush fire, ignited by the hot temperatures and gusting Santa Ana winds, rose in a billowing column high into the sky. Lani spotted an unoccupied taxi and jogged over to it. Her eyes burned and, despite her deepening sorrow, she told herself her tears were caused by the acrid air from the fire. But within the farthest reaches of her crying, pounding heart, Lani knew exactly what caused her tears. Fighting for control, hoping it would all turn out to be an extended nightmare, Lani gave the driver directions to her condominium and settled down into the back seat, no longer able to stop the sobs rising in her throat.

# 12

THE SANTA ANA winds eventually dissipated and the usual autumn temperatures returned. Mornings would often be shrouded in fog and Lani welcomed the feeling of solitude it brought as she spent the next two weeks trying to ease the pain of losing Bo. She'd tried to bury her thoughts in work but there was always the constant reminder of the sherry commercial or the office staff discussing the "big game."

She'd tried to purge the memories of the idyllic weekend in the mountains with several long, exhaustive swims in the ocean but it did no good. Charlie and the others were quick to notice the change that had come over Lani and the brittle edge she developed any time Bo's name was mentioned. They'd refrained from questioning her about it and Lani genuinely appreciated their sensitivity.

But, instead of Bo's memory growing dim with the passage of time, it intensified as Super Bowl Sunday neared. The TV news shows always had a feature on the big game. Changing the channels didn't help since all the networks carried just about the same coverage. Every pub in town had a color TV set going, tuned to interviews with players, oddsmakers, coaches, even players' wives. She couldn't walk past a newsstand without hearing the vender's radio blaring out reports on the upcoming game.

Trying to sleep at night became an ordeal. Once her eyes closed her mind raced through the course of her impassioned romance with the quarterback. Over and over again, her thoughts were drawn to images of Bo's teasing smile, his sculpted facial features, his curving lips, his flashing hazel eyes. Was it really true? she asked herself. Had she really lost him forever?

Saturday night, before the big game, everything had seemed to draw to a head. She'd felt the pressure building and now, with the Super Bowl on everyone's lips, Lani's anxiety tore at her insides. She'd turned down Charlie's offer to join him and the rest of the staff at a favorite supper club. She knew that discussion on the game and in particular about Bo, would abound and the thought of having to sit through it all, maintaining a straight face, while feeling so miserable inside, would be more than she could manage.

Lying in her bed, Lani had hoped the boring novel opened in front of her would put her to sleep. But her eyes merely stared at the pages, the words fuzzing over, her thoughts a million miles away. She closed the book and tossed it to the floor. Snapping off the light, Lani rolled onto her side and closed her eyes, hoping for once that she'd fall into a deep, calming sleep.

But it was no good. Her pulse still raced, her stomach still churned and her heart still ached. She threw back the covers and paced the room, hoping to tire herself out somehow when she suddenly decided to risk turning on the TV. She pulled a small portable set into the bedroom and tuned in to a well-worn B movie.

Might as well make the best of it, she thought, so she dished out some ice cream from the freezer, jumped back into bed, and tried to concentrate on the movie.

Somehow, Lani managed to drift into a light, uneasy sleep. But even this was no solution. She tossed and turned through the same unsettling dreams about she and Bo.

Lani awoke to find her pillow wet with perspiration, her blankets and sheets twisted in a heap on the side of the bed. Her small quartz bedside clock showed it was only five in the morning.

Wiping a hand across her brow, she got out of bed and went to the bathroom. After splashing cold water over her face, she gazed into the mirror to be met by her red-eyed image. What a night! she reflected. And now it was Sunday, the day when Bo's future plans would probably be determined. If he won the big game, he said he'd retire. But did it really matter anymore, Lani wondered while she brushed her teeth. If his decision had to be delayed until he learned the outcome of a football game, didn't that indicate where his priorities were? Didn't that mean that despite everything Lani would always come out second best to his love for football? How could she stand to see him play year after year, growing old, losing every last scrap of dignity? She rinsed and spit the mouthful of water into the basin.

This was ridiculous she realized. Here she was tormenting herself with an endless onslaught of nagging painful questions. She had to quit second-guessing herself. She needed to get out of the smothering confines of her apartment and breathe freely.

Tossing on her velour warm-up suit, sneakers, and a knit cap, Lani hurriedly left her house. She got into her Mustang and drove around the Sunset Cliffs' road, slowly moving through the thick fog rolling in from the ocean. Reaching the beach, Lani parked and strolled across the sand. The rising sun cast everything around her in a silvery glow. The lonely moan of a distant foghorn and the misty shroud gave the deserted ocean front an eerie, forlorn quality.

Reaching the wet sand, Lani broke into a medium jog. She sucked in deep lungfulls of salty air and quickened her pace. Her pounding feet splashed through the remains of a retreating wave, continuing to accelerate until she was running flat out, welcoming the burning pain in her legs, reveling in the air that brushed her face. She continued until she reached the sandstone rocks where the cliffs met the sea. Panting hard, Lani paused only briefly before clambering over the rocks, climbing past piles of mussel-encrusted seaweed until she found a dry niche in a rock overlooking a good-sized tide pool. She sat heavily into the comfortable niche and leaned back, closing her eyes, breathing deeply until her pulse and respiration rate slowed to normal.

Opening her eyes, Lani saw that the fog was lifting and in the warming sunlight, she could see several small creatures moving about in the tide pool. She focused her gaze on a crab swimming in the clear water, foraging for his breakfast. All manner of delicate plants populated this little world all to itself. How simple and complete it all seemed to Lani. It was a marked contrast to the complicated painful world she lived in.

Why couldn't things be simple like when she was a girl growing up in Hawaii. She had lived day to day, swimming in the ocean, coexisting with nature, totally uninvolved in the pressures of a modern society like the creatures in the tide pool.

A breaker smashed into the rock below her, sending up a rain of salty spray. Lani could literally feel the energy of the sea as the rocks beneath her vibrated from the force.

How could she have gotten herself into such a mess? How could she have become so vulnerable? And yet, for a few weeks, Bo had made her happier than anytime

## Conquering Embrace 171

since she was a girl growing up in Hawaii. Why did everything suddenly hinge on Bo's blind ambition? And why did Bo's proclamation of love still burn within her heart, keeping her a prisoner to the memories?

Her grandfather certainly never seemed to get so upset, so churned up inside. The gentle, wizened old man had his own view on things, to be sure. He certainly seemed to have answers to just about anything.

Lani remembered strolling through the lush rain forests of the big island hand in hand with her grandfather as he pointed out small animals, camouflaged among the thick foliage. He knew all about the plants, too, supplying her with not only their everyday names but with their ancient folk names. Lani had asked him that day why, when all around them the world was becoming more and more modern and people were using all manner of modern conveniences, did he continue to live the simple life, in a humble house, cooking on a wood stove, fishing in the old way without modern rigs. The old man smiled fondly and Lani could still see the sparkle in his eyes. They sat near a waterfall and the sun filtering through the trees made his silver-white hair seem to glow.

He began to answer her question by saying that indeed the world was filling with all kinds of wonders. When he was a little boy, there were no airplanes to speak of and now a jet could fly faster than the sound its engines made. There were skyscrapers of steel and glass, but with all these wonders how could a simple man such as himself possibly hope to make sense of it all? The only true answer he could give Lani was that life was too precious to give in to the frustrations that plagued the modern world. He had chosen instead to live life following the direction his heart told him to. If one follows the teachings of the heart, the road you travel is sure to lead to happiness, that was his message.

And what did her heart beat for now? Lani reflected sadly. Her feelings for Bo were stronger than ever, but how could she reconcile giving herself up to a man who didn't know when to quit playing a child's game before it destroyed him?

But hadn't he shown her a different dimension when he offered her advice during the tennis tournament? Lani gazed deeply into the tide pool and saw a starfish steadfastly sucking at an abalone: The abalone was just as persistently maintaining its grip on a rock, desperately clinging for its life. As she watched this silent drama, Lani knew that the starfish would eventually win out and make a meal of the abalone. But that didn't keep the little shellfish from fighting against the starfish until the very end.

And where was her competitive spirit? Lani wondered. She had let it grow lax and was giving up, without a fight. Damn it! How could she have succumbed to her feelings of grief so easily?

Logic told her it was quite possible that Bo's recent change of attitude, his blind ambition to win at all costs, could very well have been his way of getting psyched-up for the big game. Even if that weren't the case, why was Lani letting him slip away from her life by simply acquiescing and accepting her anguish as fate? Another wave crashed into the rocks and the tide pool filled up in a froth of bubbles and spray. When the water subsided, running off through the rocks, Lani saw that the starfish had been washed away and the determined abalone was still clinging to the rock, having won another chance at life, at least for the day.

Inspired by the abalone's resolve, and with her grandfather's words still echoing in her thoughts, Lani felt her competitive spirit ignite within her. She would fly to San Francisco. She would tell Bo exactly what she felt for him. He had to know that, whether or not he won the Super Bowl, she would stick by him. Lani wasn't about to let him go without a fight and somehow, she convinced herself, somehow she'd work things out between them.

Standing up, she stretched, breathed deeply, and stared

## Conquering Embrace

far out to sea. "Thank you grandfather..." she called wistfully out to the horizon before scampering down the rocks and jogging back to her car.

Lani literally flew through her front door and grabbed the phone and dialed her boss.

"Hello?" Charlie's voice was still thick from waking up.

"Charlie, I need a ticket for the Super Bowl, right away," Lani stated as she held the receiver in one hand and stripped off the jogging suit with the other.

"Lani? It's eight o'clock on Sunday morning..." He replied without hearing her question.

"I'm sorry, chief, but it's an emergency. I need a ticket for the game. I figured that if anyone can get one on such short notice it's got to be you," Lani continued, carrying the phone into the bathroom and spinning the knobs on the shower.

"Is that some kind of compliment?" he answered, a slight note of irritation in his voice.

"C'mon Charlie, I wouldn't have woken you up if it wasn't important... besides, eight's not so early," she countered while extending a hand into the shower spray to test the temperature.

"Not for a nature child like you maybe, but I was up till three this morning." he answered, still cranky.

"Charles..." Lani moaned.

"All right, don't get excited. I can tell when a woman's got to see the man of her dreams no matter how much she abuses the good nature of her boss." He laughed loudly. "If you simply can't live without being at the game with Cornell, who am I to stand in the way of true love?"

"Spare me the violins, Charlie. Can you do it?" Lani cut in, growing impatient.

"Maybe, I know a fairly reliable scalper. But it'll cost you."

"Just put it on my expense account... You're a doll Charlie, thank you," she said, breathing a sigh of relief.

"My man's usually pretty busy on the day of a game and it might take a few calls but I'll do my best, I wasn't going to do anything today anyway besides sleep and maybe get up in time to watch the game on TV. Call me back in a half an hour."

"Right and thanks again Charlie." Lani hung up and quickly called the airport to reserve a flight. They were booked solid and the chances of getting a seat from a cancellation didn't look good. Lani chose not to dwell on this setback. If there was any seat available, any seat at all, she'd get it. Resolutely hanging up the phone, she stepped into the shower.

True to his word, Charlie performed a miracle and got her a ticket. Throwing on a pair of well-fitting jeans, a cotton sweater, and a pair of low-heeled leather boots, Lani grabbed her khaki trenchcoat and flew out the door. The drive to Charlie's elegant La Jolla townhouse was mercifully quick but even so, precious time was slipping away.

She had to reach Bo in time. She couldn't let him play thinking she'd abandoned him when he needed her most.

Back on the road, it wasn't long before Lani hit the Sunday beach traffic. Her car crawled along toward the airport and Lani felt like screaming her frustrations to the throngs of teenagers, in their surfboard-topped cars, packing the highway.

Finally, Lani reached the airport and, paying the exorbitant parking fee, she dashed into the terminal. She couldn't believe her luck as a cancellation showed up on the ticket agent's computer monitor just as she reached the counter.

It was a quarter to twelve by the time Lani slumped into the seat of the commercial shuttle flight. The seemingly casual manner in which the jet's door was closed and the slow taxi into take off position was maddening.

The jet finally lifted off and, as the pilot guided the craft into a steep, smooth ascent, Lani leaned her head

## Conquering Embrace 175

against the seat and closed her eyes, wondering exactly what she'd say to Bo, hoping she'd get to the stadium on time.

The flight was only fifty minutes but it was enough time for Lani's heart to slow down so she could compose her thoughts.

The plane banked steeply for its descent and, looking out the window, Lani saw the expanse of San Francisco Bay. In the distance, the Golden Gate Bridge towered majestically over the entrance to one of nature's most breathtaking harbors. San Francisco!

Once the plane landed and Lani hustled out into the brisk ocean air wafting in from the bay, her heart began to pound again. By the time she flagged a taxi, it was already one-thirty. She was too late for the kick-off.

"Candlestick Park," she directed to the driver. He turned his head back to Lani and, with raised eyebrows and a smile he said, "Super Bowl, huh? I can't promise there will be much of a game left by the time we get there, this traffic's murder..."

"Doesn't matter," Lani said, staring out the window, "I've got to get there."

"Sure, m'am. Might as well relax and enjoy the drive, it'll be a long one." He sighed and pulled away from the passenger terminal.

The cabbie was right. Traffic was at a near standstill. His small transistor radio, hanging from a knob on the dashboard, was tuned to the game. A nervous knot twisted tighter and tighter inside Lani's chest as she heard the game progressing, passing the first half, the start of the second, halfway through the third quarter and still the taxi merely crawled toward the stadium.

The Lions and Dallas Mustangs were trading touchdowns and with each score the cabbie's radio blasted out the roar of the crowd and the announcers' excited commentary.

With the game clock ticking away Lani felt her insides churning more and more with each precious second lost.

Overhead, the deep blue sky filled with clouds and what had started as a brisk, sunny morning was now becoming an ever darkening, chilly afternoon. A few errant sprinkles hit the windshield and the cabbie switched on the wipers. But the darkening sky didn't diminish Lani's resolve to reach Bo and tell him how much she loved him, how committed she was to working things out between them.

The Mustangs scored to pull ahead and a wall of deafening sound rose and crackled through the air, drowning out everything else. Looking out the window, Lani could see the upper rim of the stadium, half a mile away. The crowd's roar sent her blood rushing and her anxiety mounting to the limit.

The cabbie continued to inch the taxi forward and finally a traffic officer waved them through the parking entrance. The cabbie barely had time to stop before Lani tossed him a twenty dollar bill and dashed off on foot for the stadium entrance.

Everywhere, someone had a radio tuned to the game: cops, ticket takers, concessionaires. There were only a couple of minutes left in the fourth and final quarter.

Lani held out her ticket to a nearby ticket taker but he merely smiled and waved her through without bothering to take her ticket. The crowd noise was a constant hum occasionally bursting into piercing cheers. It would probably take at least fifteen minutes to reach her seat and right now that's the last place Lani wanted to be.

Spotting a stadium guard, Lani approached him. "Which way is the players' dressing rooms," she asked hurriedly.

"Keep heading down and around, then take stairway *L*."

"Thanks," Lani said and dashed off.

"Hey, you can't...it's for officials only," the man replied, realizing his mistake.

"Press!" Lani yelled back over her shoulder and continued in the direction he indicated.

A nearby souvenir vendor's radio announced that the Lions' quarterback was down. A loud, collective moan from the crowd followed. Lani halted in mid-stride, feeling an icy chill shiver through her back as she realized that Bo might be hurt. The radio shifted to a commercial.

Lani continued her rush toward stairway *L*. She passed a hotdog stand and paused to hear the rest of the radio report. Bo was indeed injured. It appeared to be his shoulder. He was leaving the game but he was walking under his own power. The crowd began the customary applause for a fallen player. Lani spotted the stairway. She reached the cement corridor leading down to the bowels of the stadium just as the final gun went off. All around her, fans suddenly emerged from the stadium tunnels, rushing to beat the traffic. It was clear from their jabber that the Lions had lost.

Everyone around her was jostling, celebrating, or lining up for a last-minute souvenir, or hot dog; arguing over the game. No one seemed to pay any attention to Lani so she continued following the signs until she reached field level. She heard a loud cacophony coming from her left. Lani felt her heart pounding as she realized she was approaching the door to the players' dressing rooms. There must have been a couple of hundred people gathered around the door as a quartet of burly stadium security guards held them at bay.

Lani reached the periphery and pulled on the sleeve of a man peering over the throng. "Is this the Lions' locker room?"

"You got it," he yelled over his shoulder without looking back.

It seemed like everyone was trying to gain access to the locker room. How could she shove her way past this horde of reporters, fans, and who knew what else? Nevertheless, Lani hadn't come all the way for nothing and taking a deep breath, she hunched her shoulders and plunged into the crowd. Shoving and squirming, she slowly made her way to the front of the crowd, only to halt before an astonishing sight. Sheryl Canning was standing next to her, screaming at a guard, demanding to be let in to see Cornell. He was her client, she said, and she had to know how badly he was hurt. But the guard remained indifferent to her demands.

Lani moved up to the guard and whispered into his ear.

"Officer, my name's Leilani Richards. I'm here to see Bo Cornell," Lani stated, trying to sound calm and with more than a hint of respect for the abused and overworked guard.

"What?" He yelled back over the throng.

"Leilani Richards... I'm here to see Bo Cornell. I'm sure he left word..." Lani yelled back.

"Sorry, ma'am, nobody's allowed in until the team spokesman gives the word."

Lani could hear Sheryl still yelling at another guard getting nowhere but making a big fuss nevertheless. Lani was just about ready to resign herself to waiting it out with the rest of them when another guard shoved his way to her. "Miss Richards, I heard you say that was your name?"

"Yes?" Lani replied, trying to read his face.

"Cornell left word that if you showed up we were to let you in, whatever... C'mon..." he offered, putting a protective arm around her shoulder and nodding to his partner that it was okay.

Lani suddenly felt her spirits lift. It was as if a huge weight had been taken off her shoulders. She turned back to see Sheryl. The woman was outraged; incredulity washed over her red face. With a quiet smile, Lani ducked beneath the guard's arm as he held the door open for her.

Inside the team dressing room all was silent except for some idle shuffling and barely perceptible mumbling. In front of one dressing stall, Lani saw two players in an intimate conversation, one looping an arm around the shoulders of the other, trying to ease the pain each felt over the disappointing loss. So this is what it's like, Lani thought to herself, taking in the sad faces, bowed heads. They were all pictures of frustration.

The guard led her past several more dressing stalls, stepping lightly over the litter of disgarded pads, helmets, lines of tape, until they reached Bo. He was sitting on a stool, his back propped against the rear of the dressing stall. With a tip of his cap, the guard moved off, leaving them alone.

Lani gasped involuntarily as she noticed the huge ice pack fixed to Bo's shoulder with an elastic bandage. Flecks of blood mingled with the dirt on his uniform. His face, covered in sweat, a few blades of grass and chalk from the field markings, sported a terrible looking black eye.

Slowly opening his eyes, Bo leveled his gaze at her. He looked terrible and Lani's hand clutched her throat as she paled at the sight. But Bo responded by breaking into a wide, lazy grin, while his eyes flashed his joy at seeing her. "Lani, you're the best thing I've seen all day," he drawled in fatigue.

"Oh, Bo. I tried to get here to see you before the game, to let you know I wasn't abandoning you..." she exclaimed sitting on a stool next to him and placing a gentle hand against his cheek. "How bad are you hurt? The radio said..."

"It's nothing, really," he replied soothingly, taking her hand and bringing it to his lips.

"But Bo, your shoulder," Lani continued, unable to hide her concern.

"Just a bruise... I don't even need this," he replied, unwrapping the ice bag and tossing it to the floor. He stole a glance into a small mirror hanging in the stall. "Oh, brother. I look like I just got out of a cage full of bears." He laughed.

But it obviously hurt more than he let on because he suddenly winced and touched a tentative finger to the ugly purple bruise below his eye. Then, looking intently at her, searching her sober features, he said, "C'mon, let's go someplace where we can be alone." He rose, taking her hand, and led her quietly out of the dressing room, down a hall. Lani followed obediently, anxious for the chance to spell out her feelings for him, eager to make him realize how willing she was to work it out between them. The feel of his strong, sure grasp made her fingers tingle and a nervous shiver traced a path up her arm. Her heart continued to beat rapidly.

He tried a door. It was locked but the next one yielded and he looked inside. "This looks good," he said, pulling her in after him and closing the door. He flipped on the light to reveal rows and rows of football equipment hung on hooks. Tables were piled high with uniforms, parkas, socks.

"Bo, I'm sorry about the other day, when you asked me to come to the game. I feel...I feel like I let you down," she began, her voice thick with emotion.

Bo reached out and circled his arms around her waist and turned her to face him directly, towering over her, a massive figure in his uniform. "That's enough, Lani. I don't care about anything except that you're here with me now," he stated evenly, staring deeply into her eyes.

She suddenly was at a loss for words. She had so much to say it was hard to know where to begin. Then her grandfather's words filtered back through her thoughts. Lani had to follow the yearnings of her heart and right now it was beating a mile a minute for Bo. She began tentatively but determined to let him know how she felt. "Those men, your teammates, they seemed...so sad. I guess I never really understood how emotional football really was, how intense."

"Yeah, it is intense. Enough to make men put everything they have, their hearts, their bodies, everything, into one hour of all-out fury once a week. Crazy, huh?" he reflected, his tone filled with irony.

"I don't know, a lot of things seem crazy to me right now," Lani answered.

"You still think football's a kid's game," he goaded, his bushy eyebrows knitting.

"I admit I judged too quickly," she offered, lowering her eyes slightly, "but it's not easy seeing the man I love punish himself for something that's so removed from what the rest of us do."

Bo's eyebrows arched in response to her proclamation and he stared at her. Lani had put her feelings on the line. It was too late to stop now, she realized, and she returned Bo's stare, hoping he'd read her sincerity.

She pressed herself closer to him, biting her lower lip nervously. "I don't think I can go on without you, Bo. Half the time I can't sleep at night thinking about you. I don't want to see you getting hurt, but I love you and I need you. If football is so important to you, then I won't stand in the way..." She shifted her eyes over his features, staring intently into his eyes, trying to sense his reaction. "You decide what's best for you, Bo. I won't stop you, but I don't want to be without you either."

He ran his hand softly over her hair and leaned down so close that his breath blew hot across her cheeks. "Does that mean you won't run away from me... even if I want to play again next year?"

Lani's lips quivered anxiously; her heart beat furiously against his chest. "It means that I want you, Bo, and whatever it takes to keep you, I'll do it."

His features softened and his eyes hazed over. "You don't know how much it means to me to hear you say that, Lani," he said before breaking into a broad grin. "But you know what, darling? I've already decided about next year. I'm just too old to compete with these fast, hungry kids coming into the game. I've had it with the bruises, the long nights pouring over game films, studying the other team's defense. It's time this ol' boy got into something new."

Lani could hardly believe her ears. A mist filled her eyes and warmth suddenly flooded through her body.

"You really mean it, darling?" she asked, her voice wavering tremulously.

"Of course I mean it," he replied, smiling, his hazel eyes dancing in amusement.

It was what she'd hoped for all along and Bo's words filled Lani's eyes with tears of joy. But with all that had gone on between them during the last few months, she had to be sure. "The Lions lost today, Bo. You won't change your mind later and regret retiring? You won't suddenly start thinking you can't leave the game a loser?" she asked, risking everything as she prayed for the final commitment from the man she loved so desperately.

But he merely stared at her for a moment and then his smile softened as he replied in a subdued tone, "I'm not a loser, darling. I've won you and that's all that matters." He sealed the proclamation by gently pressing his lips against hers and Lani melted, throwing her arms around his neck, leaning up on her tiptoes to drink in his kiss. Bo's protective embrace thrilled and comforted Lani and a warm flush spread over her from head to toe. Pressing her lips tightly against his, tears of joy coursed slowly down her cheeks, over their mated mouths.

He pulled back slightly and, reaching a finger up to wipe away an errant tear, he broke into a warm little smile. "Does this mean you'll help me with my new career?"

She laughed giddily. "You bet! I'll get your name into every household in America."

"You might be flirting with a conflict of interest, Lani," he teased, kissing away another tear from the corner of her eye.

"I don't know what you mean, Bo," she replied, reading the amusement in his face.

"Well, you see it won't just be my name you'll be promoting, darling. It'll be *our* name," he replied, flashing his broadest smile.

Her heart seemed to skip a beat as Bo left no doubt as to his intentions. "Oh, yes, Bo, yes..." she whis-

## Conquering Embrace 183

pered, but he silenced her with a kiss. Lani felt faint with unbridled joy as she met his sensual kiss with her own. From the dressing room a coach's loud voice projected into the utility room as he lead the team in a cheer. The muffled voices of the players followed as they congratulated themselves on the end of a fine season. As their rhythmic chanting continued, it was as if they were cheering for Bo and Lani. But her thoughts were a million miles away, swirling in a paradise with the man she knew she would love forever.

____ 06540-4 FROM THE TORRID PAST #49 Ann Cristy
____ 06544-7 RECKLESS LONGING #50 Daisy Logan
____ 05851-3 LOVE'S MASQUERADE #51 Lillian Marsh
____ 06148-4 THE STEELE HEART #52 Jocelyn Day
____ 06422-X UNTAMED DESIRE #53 Beth Brookes
____ 06651-6 VENUS RISING #54 Michelle Roland
____ 06595-1 SWEET VICTORY #55 Jena Hunt
____ 06575-7 TOO NEAR THE SUN #56 Aimée Duvall
____ 05625-1 MOURNING BRIDE #57 Lucia Curzon
____ 06411-4 THE GOLDEN TOUCH #58 Robin James
____ 06596-X EMBRACED BY DESTINY #59 Simone Hadary
____ 06660-5 TORN ASUNDER #60 Ann Cristy
____ 06573-0 MIRAGE #61 Margie Michaels
____ 06650-8 ON WINGS OF MAGIC #62 Susanna Collins
____ 05816-5 DOUBLE DECEPTION #63 Amanda Troy
____ 06675-3 APOLLO'S DREAM #64 Claire Evans
____ 06680-X THE ROGUE'S LADY #69 Anne Devon
____ 06689-3 SWEETER THAN WINE #78 Jena Hunt
____ 06690-7 SAVAGE EDEN #79 Diane Crawford
____ 06692-3 THE WAYWARD WIDOW #81 Anne Mayfield
____ 06693-1 TARNISHED RAINBOW #82 Jocelyn Day
____ 06694-X STARLIT SEDUCTION #83 Anne Reed
____ 06695-8 LOVER IN BLUE #84 Aimée Duvall

All of the above titles are $1.75 per copy

*Available at your local bookstore or return this form to:*

**SECOND CHANCE AT LOVE**
*Book Mailing Service*
*P.O. Box 690, Rockville Centre, NY 11571*

Please send me the titles checked above. I enclose _____
Include $1.00 for postage and handling if one book is ordered; 50¢ per book for two or more. California, Illinois, New York and Tennessee residents please add sales tax.

NAME _____

ADDRESS _____

CITY _____ STATE/ZIP _____

(allow six weeks for delivery)                           S 41b

___ 06696-6 **THE FAMILIAR TOUCH #85** Lynn Lawrence
___ 06697-4 **TWILIGHT EMBRACE #86** Jennifer Rose
___ 06698-2 **QUEEN OF HEARTS #87** Lucia Curzon
___ 06850-0 **PASSION'S SONG #88** Johanna Phillips
___ 06851-9 **A MAN'S PERSUASION #89** Katherine Granger
___ 06852-7 **FORBIDDEN RAPTURE #90** Kate Nevins
___ 06853-5 **THIS WILD HEART #91** Margarett McKean
___ 06854-3 **SPLENDID SAVAGE #92** Zandra Colt
___ 06855-1 **THE EARL'S FANCY #93** Charlotte Hines
___ 06858-6 **BREATHLESS DAWN #94** Susanna Collins
___ 06859-4 **SWEET SURRENDER #95** Diana Mars
___ 06860-8 **GUARDED MOMENTS #96** Lynn Fairfax
___ 06861-6 **ECSTASY RECLAIMED #97** Brandy LaRue
___ 06862-4 **THE WIND'S EMBRACE #98** Melinda Harris
___ 06863-2 **THE FORGOTTEN BRIDE #99** Lillian Marsh
___ 06864-0 **A PROMISE TO CHERISH #100** LaVyrle Spencer
___ 06865-9 **GENTLE AWAKENING #101** Marianne Cole
___ 06866-7 **BELOVED STRANGER #102** Michelle Roland
___ 06867-5 **ENTHRALLED #103** Ann Cristy
___ 06869-1 **DEFIANT MISTRESS #105** Anne Devon
___ 06870-5 **RELENTLESS DESIRE #106** Sandra Brown
___ 06871-3 **SCENES FROM THE HEART #107** Marie Charles
___ 06872-1 **SPRING FEVER #108** Simone Hadary
___ 06873-X **IN THE ARMS OF A STRANGER #109** Deborah Joyce
___ 06874-8 **TAKEN BY STORM #110** Kay Robbins
___ 06899-3 **THE ARDENT PROTECTOR #111** Amanda Kent
___ 07200-1 **A LASTING TREASURE #112** Cally Hughes $1.95

All of the above titles are $1.75 per copy except where noted

---

Available at your local bookstore or return this form to:

**SECOND CHANCE AT LOVE**
Book Mailing Service
P.O. Box 690, Rockville Centre, NY 11571

Please send me the titles checked above. I enclose _____
Include $1.00 for postage and handling if one book is ordered; 50¢ per book for two or more. California, Illinois, New York and Tennessee residents please add sales tax.

NAME _____

ADDRESS _____

CITY _____ STATE/ZIP _____
(allow six weeks for delivery)

SK-41c

_____ 07201-X **RESTLESS TIDES** #113 Kelly Adams $1.95
_____ 07202-8 **MOONLIGHT PERSUASION** #114 Sharon Stone $1.95
_____ 07203-6 **COME WINTER'S END** #115 Claire Evans $1.95
_____ 07204-4 **LET PASSION SOAR** #116 Sherry Carr $1.95
_____ 07205-2 **LONDON FROLIC** #117 Josephine Janes $1.95
_____ 07206-0 **IMPRISONED HEART** #118 Jasmine Craig $1.95
_____ 07207-9 **THE MAN FROM TENNESSEE** #119 Jeanne Grant $1.95
_____ 07208-7 **LAUGH WITH ME, LOVE WITH ME** #120 Lee Damon $1.95
_____ 07209-5 **PLAY IT BY HEART** #121 Vanessa Valcour $1.95
_____ 07210-9 **SWEET ABANDON** #122 Diana Mars $1.95
_____ 07211-7 **THE DASHING GUARDIAN** #123 Lucia Curzon $1.95
_____ 07212-5 **SONG FOR A LIFETIME** #124 Mary Haskell $1.95
_____ 07213-3 **HIDDEN DREAMS** #125 Johanna Phillips $1.95
_____ 07214-1 **LONGING UNVEILED** #126 Meredith Kingston $1.95
_____ 07215-X **JADE TIDE** #127 Jena Hunt $1.95
_____ 07216-8 **THE MARRYING KIND** #128 Jocelyn Day $1.95
_____ 07217-6 **CONQUERING EMBRACE** #129 Ariel Tierney $1.95

*Available at your local bookstore or return this form to:*

**SECOND CHANCE AT LOVE**
*Book Mailing Service*
*P.O. Box 690, Rockville Centre, NY 11571*

Please send me the titles checked above. I enclose _____
Include $1.00 for postage and handling if one book is ordered; 50¢ per book for two or more. California, Illinois, New York and Tennessee residents please add sales tax.

NAME _____

ADDRESS _____

CITY _____ STATE/ZIP _____
(allow six weeks for delivery)

# WHAT READERS SAY ABOUT SECOND CHANCE AT LOVE BOOKS

"Your books are the greatest!"
—*M. N., Carteret, New Jersey**

"I have been reading romance novels for quite some time, but the SECOND CHANCE AT LOVE books are the most enjoyable."
—*P. R., Vicksburg, Mississippi**

"I enjoy SECOND CHANCE [AT LOVE] more than any books that I have read and I do read a lot."
—*J. R., Gretna, Louisiana**

"I really think your books are exceptional . . . I read Harlequin and Silhouette and although I still like them, I'll buy your books over theirs. SECOND CHANCE [AT LOVE] is more interesting and holds your attention and imagination with a better story line . . ."
—*J. W., Flagstaff, Arizona**

"I've read many romances, but yours take the 'cake'!"
—*D. H., Bloomsburg, Pennsylvania**

"Have waited ten years for *good* romance books. Now I have them."
—*M. P., Jacksonville, Florida**

*Names and addresses available upon request